AF285228

I can honestly say I've never read anything quite like this book. It's funny, ironic, and thought-provoking, all of it tinged with a bit of dark drama. With such a complex plot this book could so easily have gone wrong – leaving the reader bewildered by the fanciful turn of events, but instead, the author has done a masterful job of taking us along on a great ride as the protagonist, Eberhardt Walker a writer who, almost as an aside, goes about ridding the city of brutal criminals, in between having fascinating philosophical conversations with great literary characters. I enjoyed this book from beginning to end, so *The 92 Year Old Lady Who Made Me Steal a Dead Man's Car* is an easy book to recommend.

Marquita Herald, Author

To the many fictional characters who accompanied me throughout my life. The events revealed in this book could not have happened without their contributions.

Fred Schäfer

The 92-Year-Old Lady Who Made Me Steal a Dead Man's Car

A thrilling and seriously funny novel

The 92-Year-Old Lady Who Made Me Steal a Dead Man's Car

Copyright © 2013 Paul Friedrich Schäfer (Fred Schäfer)

ISBN 9783752609998
Originally published by Condor Books
Herstellung und Verlag: BoD – Books on Demand, Norderstedt
Bibliografische Information der Deutschen Nationalbibliothek: Die Deutsche Nationalbibliothek verzeichnet diese Publikation in der Deutschen Nationalbibliografie; detaillierte bibliografische Daten sind im Internet über dnb.dnb.de abrufbar.

Fred Schäfer asserts the moral right to be identified as the author of this work. All rights reserved. No part of this book may be reproduced in any manner without the definite written consent of the author, except in the case of brief excerpts in reviews or articles. All inquiries should be directed to the Publisher.
This novel is a work of fiction. Names, characters, places, events and incidents are either the work of the author's imagination or are used fictitiously.

About Fred Schäfer

Fred Schäfer was born in the south of Germany and left home at the age of nineteen. A few years later he discovered the world of literature.

Two of his books, *The Short and Wonderful Life of Henry Hemingway* and *Travelling with Maria*, provide insight into the early years of his life. *The Mysterious Man* adds to the picture, although not entirely, because *The Mysterious Man* is a novel, not an autobiography. Or is it both? A book in which reality and fiction merge? Fred Schäfer's multilayered autobiography is entitled *Identity Uncertain*.

At the age of thirty-six, the author and his family moved to Australia, where they reside today. He has worked as an engineer and IT manager, then became a professional speaker making a name for himself presenting business and personal development seminars. During those years, he wrote two nonfiction books: *The Solution Within Yourself* and *Success, Money and You*. A few years later he published the essence of his seminars in his third nonfiction book, *How to Make Great Things Happen in YOUR LIFE*.

Fred Schäfer's heart belongs to the world of literature, which to him means fiction. He has written ten novels, three in German and seven in English, and one novella. A short description of his writings can be found at the end of this book. His English novels are:

Unedited Realities: Journeys beyond time and infinity
Having Coffee and Cake with the Devil in Chicago
An Almighty Conspiracy
The Invention of the Big Bang
The 92-Year-Old Lady Who Made Me Steal a Dead Man's Car
The Mysterious Man
Don't Mention the FBI and
Invitation to a Former Girlfriend's Wedding (a novella)

The 92-Year-Old Lady Who Made Me Steal a Dead Man's Car, clearly, is Fred Schäfer's most imaginative literary fiction novel. The author demonstrates his creative power to an almost unimaginable degree. Literary characters from the books of his heroes come alive and attempt something, which would make their authors, if they knew about it, scream in horror or roll over in their graves.

Books by Fred Schäfer

A short description of each book can be found at the end of this novel.

www.amazon.com/author/fs

Identity Uncertain: An Autobiography
Unedited Realities: Journeys beyond time and infinity
Having Coffee and Cake with the Devil in Chicago
Don't Mention the FBI
The Mysterious Man
The 92-Year-Old Lady Who Made Me Steal a Dead Man's Car
The Invention of the Big Bang
An Almighty Conspiracy
The Short and Wonderful Life of Henry Hemingway
Travelling with Maria: Embracing Life
How to Make Great Things Happen in YOUR LIFE
The Solution Within Yourself
Success, Money and You
Das Zimmer zur Welt
Die andere Wirklichkeit
Die Beeinflussung des jungen Jakob Berg durch Henry Miller
Drei idealistische Bücher mit provozierendem Inhalt
Der Berg hat aufgehört zu schwingen
Zwischenbilanz
Die Aufzeichnungen

Table of Contents

PART 1: 9
Introducing the old lady, the dead man and myself

PART 2: 55
Love, sex and legal complications

PART 3: 99
The twenty five literary characters and time travelling

PART 4: 129
A happy ending for Lady Brett Ashley and Jake Barnes

PART 5: 157
The unanimous decision of the philosophy aficionados

PART 6: 195
The 92-year-old lady and her
91-year-old lover who killed himself at 61

Author's Note   213

Principal literary characters   215

Books by Fred Schäfer   217

Note for fiction fans

A list of the books, authors and literary characters mentioned on the following pages can be found at the end of this novel. This list is also included in the Table of Contents. See: *Principal literary characters*.

To enjoy this novel, there is no need to be familiar with these works of fiction. The list mentioned above has been included for the benefit and convenience of fiction fans.

PART 1:

Introducing the old lady, the dead man and myself

1

The old lady and I stepped onto the pedestrian crossing. We didn't know each other and hardly paid attention to each other. The pedestrian light had been on green and changed to red shortly after we had left the safety of the footpath. After I had reached the other side of the street, the traffic lights for the cars changed. A moment later, I heard the aggressive sound of a horn and the abusive voice of a male. "Damn old bitch, get out of my way, or I'll run you over!" The man's language was more colourful, but there is no need to repeat word by word what he said.

I turned around and saw the old lady standing in the middle of the street in front of an old and rusty looking Ford. The Ford's driver was hanging out of the window screaming and honking the horn of his car like a madman. The old lady stood calmly. She had turned towards the aggressive driver. Cars were passing on her left and right. I wanted to run back and help her. Just when I was about to step onto the street, a man grabbed my shoulder and pulled me back. He probably saved my life. Cars were passing in front of me like bullets. The old lady and the old Ford looked like islands in the middle of a fast-flowing river; an angry river full of big pieces of junk in its torrent.

I could see the lady trying to say something to the young driver, but I doubt he could hear her. There was a hell of noise; the traffic, the sound of the horn, and the angry driver's yelling combined to the kind of racket I suspect Neil Diamond was referring to in his song *What A Beautiful Noise*, except in this instance, it wasn't beautiful. I think Neil would have agreed with me on that.

The old lady walked a few steps towards the car and smashed one of the car's front lights with her walking stick.

What a woman! I thought.

It was 5:30 pm and peak hour traffic in Manhattan. I was waiting for a gap in the traffic so that I could run to the old woman and assist her. It didn't look good. Most of the cars were driving above the speed limit. I saw the angry young man getting out of his car. He was yelling and swearing and gesticulating as if there was no tomorrow. As it turned out, there was no tomorrow for him.

He stepped out of his car right in front of a passing truck. The truck hit him, and the angry man was thrown forward and sidewise at the same time. He hit the ground and didn't move; killed instantly. The truck that had hit him continued down the street, while the young man's body remained motionless beside the old lady.

I don't know what got into me. I ran onto the street, completely ignoring the traffic, and the next thing I knew, I found myself beside the old lady and the dead body. One look confirmed that the man was definitely beyond hope. His skull had been crushed, his brain oozing out between the cracks.

The old lady looked at me, with an almost inquisitive look on her face. I looked at her and said, "Let me help you."

"What do you suggest?" she asked.

Suggest? I thought. Why does she think I am suggesting something? "Just to get you off the street," I replied.

The traffic was still speeding past us on either side. If there was a gap, I could carry her. Maybe the best thing would be to wait for the traffic lights to change and the traffic to stop. I was just about to say that when I heard her call, "Come. Hurry up!"

When I looked at the spot beside me where she had been a few seconds earlier, I realized she had walked away and was in the process of opening the passenger door of the rusty Ford in front of us. She opened the door and sat down in the passenger's seat. For a moment I was inclined to run after her, but changed my mind and went to the driver's side and sat down.

"Let's go," she said.

"Let's go?! What do you mean?"

"You can drive a car, can't you? Let's get away from here. What are you waiting for?" She smiled at me. Within a fraction of a second, I realized three things: she was very old, at least ninety, she had sparkling, bright eyes, young eyes actually, and she displayed a charismatic beauty of a kind I had never noticed before in an elderly person.

The car's engine had been running the entire time. I put the car in gear, turned the steering wheel to the right to avoid the body in front of the car, and a few seconds later was driving an old car with an old lady as my passenger. In the meantime, the traffic lights had changed once more. I found myself in the middle of the crossing and could see and hear cars coming, their horns blasting on my left and right. I pushed down the accelerator pedal as hard as I could. The old Ford was impressively well-tuned and obliged at once. A few seconds later I felt like someone who had just managed to escape by the width of a hair from an avalanche.

"Well done," my passenger said.

"We left the scene of an accident, a man was killed, and you made me steal his car. You call that well done?"

"Would anything have changed if we had stayed?" she asked. "And as far as the car is concerned, he won't need it anymore."

Very logical, I thought. It's just that not everybody would see it her way. Besides, the authorities are not likely to give her a hard time. She is not driving the car, she didn't steal it, I did, and anyway, they won't put an old woman in jail.

"I'm Irene Sonntag," she said.

"Nice to meet you, Irene," I replied. "I'm Eberhardt Walker."

"How old are you, Eberhardt?"

"Thirty-four."

"You look quite handsome and fit."

"Thank you."

"Are you married?"

I looked at her. Why on earth would she like to know that?

As if she had read my thoughts, she said, "I am asking because if you are not tied down by a relationship, I have a proposition for you."

2

I wasn't in a relationship. The woman I had been with for the past five years had left me a few weeks earlier. We weren't married but we lived together in the same apartment. For all intents and purposes, we were married, but things just weren't what they used to be anymore. In all the years we were together, we had kept separate bank accounts and had clear understandings of how to divide our belongings.

It was on a Sunday evening that she said to me, "We've reached a fork in the road. What do you think, should we go in different directions?"

"You one direction, and I the other?" I asked just to be sure I understood her.

She nodded.

"I'll miss you," I said.

"No, you won't."

She was right, and we both knew it. We wouldn't miss each other, except, perhaps, in the bedroom. We were both down-to-earth people. And for the past year or so, the only emotional events between us occurred every Wednesday and Friday evening. Whenever we could, we kept those evenings free for sex. Sex had been good until the end, everything else had slipped into insignificance.

She made heaps of money as an architect and I made enough money as a freelancer, writing a novel now and again. For a few years, we were genuinely interested in each other's activities. I studied her plans and visited the buildings she had designed, she read my articles and novels. We talked about architecture and literature, and for a while it seemed that life could happily go on like that forever.

We also shared a part-time occupation. We did undesirable things to bad people who were beyond the reach of the law: mainly violent, vicious and sadistic rapists. It is a sad fact that most sex crimes are not reported to the police. The victims – girls and women of any age – are often too afraid to go to the police, even too afraid to talk to their friends, parents, or partners about what happened to them.

I found out about these sad events regularly through my TCs, which stands for Tough Contacts, a kind of network that had established itself a few years before mine and Ella's five years of togetherness.

The TCs stuff sounds more sophisticated than it really is. In my early years as a writer, I gave talks and presented seminars to hundreds of charitable organizations and groups of people who were struggling with life for one reason or another. I'm talking about people who lived in New York's socially and economically destitute neighborhoods; the slums and crime-ridden areas of the city. My seminars were about nearly everything under the sun, but mainly about human misery and injustices, and how one can cope with it. My approach was simple: *when things go wrong, find a reason to laugh*. A bit too simple? Definitely. But somehow it worked. I often asked people to talk about something that had recently gone wrong in their lives. Most people were happy to share their challenges and miseries.

I remember a woman who complained bitterly about her boss. He was very arrogant and rude; an asshole, really. "What can I do?" she said. "What can I do? I need that job, I need the money." The entire group discussed what she could do. Some people suggested she should kill the bastard. This would be one way of fixing the problem, I agreed, but the consequences would be no laughing matter. The challenge was to find a humorous way of dealing with her terrible situation. In the end, we all agreed that she had to talk to him and tell him how he made her feel. In the past, she had always kept silent when he humiliated her.

We had half an hour of good fun. One person in the group played the asshole boss and another person – and we changed these roles several times – played the woman. The things people said to the boss were hilarious. Everybody tried to be more aggressive, rude and funnier than the person before. The poor woman who had to live with that boss would lose her job in a minute if she ever said what the players suggested, but the exercise changed her perspective. Finally, I had a go at playing the victim, which everyone was eager to see. The guy who played the bad boss said things like: "You are absolutely useless. Even the simplest things you do, you can't do right. You are a waste of space."

I replied calmly, "What you're saying is rude, aggressive, and it hurts."

For a moment there was silence. The man who played the bad boss, and who earlier in the game could always think of something to say, was searching for words. I could see it.

Then he said: "What do you mean, rude, aggressive, and it hurts?"

I said: "The way you talk to me is rude, aggressive, and hurts."

"No it's not!" the boss yelled. "How else do you expect me to talk to you?"

"Not rudely and not aggressively," I replied calmly.

"Give me an example! What do you mean?"

"Just don't be rude, aggressive, or hurt me. Please. That's all."

It went on like this for a little longer, and I explained my approach. Tell the wrongdoer what you feel in one simple, straightforward message, and keep repeating that message. Don't change it. Don't defend what you said. Don't get involved in a discussion and side issues. Just repeat again and again calmly and politely that simple message about how you feel.

This is one way to make arrogant and aggressive people slow down and think. It works often, but not always. But even if it doesn't work, the victims usually feel proud that they have stood up for themselves.

On a few occasions, I learned that my attempts to create comedy out of people's misery changed their lives for the better. There was a couple in their mid-twenties, the man was a bit of an alcoholic, and the woman once thought that when they were married, his drinking would stop. Of course, it didn't. In fact, it got worse. They were both in my seminar, and she bitterly complained about him. About the money he wasted on booze and the noise he made when he was drunk. In classic Albert Ellis style, I told her that the problem was not her husband, the problem rested with her. "Your husband," I said, "is an alcoholic and behaves exactly the way alcoholics behave. They are drunk, they waste money, and they make a lot of noise. That's how they are. For you to expect something else of your alcoholic husband is the problem. He's okay. As long as he is an alcoholic, it's your expectation of him that needs to change."

She looked at me surprised before she asked, "Are saying he's a good alcoholic?"

I couldn't help but laugh and replied, "You couldn't wish yourself a better one."

"So what are my options?"

"You have at least two options. You can accept him as he is and stop complaining. Or you can separate and seek a divorce."

"Or I could join him and get drunk, waste money, and we make noise together."

"I hadn't thought of that," I laughed, "but yes, that's definitely another option."

And that was exactly what she did.

Interestingly, and this is something I found out a year or so later, her husband wasn't impressed by her decision. One alcoholic in the family, he reasoned, was enough.

They were two intelligent people. As far as I know, they are still married and no longer drink at all.

Most of the time, I suspect the people who attended my talks had two hours of fun; beyond that, everything stayed largely the same. I thought that was okay, and people seemed to agree. Whether they agreed consciously or subconsciously, I don't know. If they hadn't had fun, I guess they wouldn't have returned for another two hours of laughter interspersed with the occasional piece of wisdom.

But why am I telling you this? I got to know lots of people who lived difficult lives. Over the years, some of them stayed in contact with me, phoning me once in a while. Sometimes they invited me to parties, other times I was asked to give a talk for ten or twenty minutes, which often turned into an hour.

I turned up in cafés, pubs, parks, or street corners where I knew I would find some of my former seminar participants. I respected and loved these people, and some of them must have noticed that. They were the ones who stayed in contact with me. One day one of them said, "We are your Tough Contacts," Maybe this sounds bigger than what it was. On the other hand, thinking about it, it was a big thing; these people trusted me and I trusted them. Trust is paramount.

It was through these contacts that I learned about crimes that were never reported to the police. I'm talking about serious cases of rape; brutal cases in which the victims were often emotionally damaged beyond help for the rest of their lives. Other unreported crimes that I learned about were related to drugs, domestic abuse, burglaries…

I don't know what it is that makes me hate rapists, especially the brutal and vicious ones. I mean, *really hate*. If a man beats up a woman and I hear about it, I want to beat up that man and I have done that on more than one occasion. But when someone tells me about rape, that's when something within me snaps and shatters, and I turn into a different man.

When I met Ella and told her about my part-time job a few months into our relationship. She said, without hesitation, "There's something we have in common."

"What?" I asked, surprised, "Do you also hate and hunt rapists?"

"From now on, *yes!*" she replied emphatically.

So, there you have it: sex was one thing, our part-time job was the other thing that kept our relationship going longer than it should have.

What we did to rapists was bad; serious crimes in themselves, and you would think that sometimes we should have felt guilty about what we did. At least, when I think about it rationally, I think that we should have felt at least… well, remorseful or uncomfortable. But we didn't. What we did always seemed like the right thing to do.

I realize of course, to call hunting and punishing bad people a part-time occupation seems wrong. It sounds cold. We probably should have felt bad about that as well. Maybe I should not admit to it, not even today. But what can I say?

I don't want you to get the wrong impression. Neither Ella nor I enjoyed what we did to these people. Our feelings were rather neutral about the punishment we dished out. There was no hate, happiness, or satisfaction.

I hate rapists, yes, but I didn't have positive feelings about punishing them. I just saw it as a job that had to be done. Somebody had to do it.

We did it in a considered way. For a start, there was no blood. We had chemicals at our disposal.

I looked at it this way: a rapist is a bit like a viciously barking dog in the neighborhood, only much worse and with one important difference. To stop the dog from barking, you don't have to do to the animal what we did to rapists. You talk to the dog's owner and convince him that they have to do something about their dog. Only if that doesn't work, you deal with the dog directly. You hate the barking dog, and the barking gets on your nerves. At the same time though, you're sensible enough to understand that it is not the dog's fault that it is a ferociously barking creature. The dog didn't wake up one morning and decide that from now on, it would terrorize the neighborhood.

A rapist didn't wake up one morning and decide to be a rapist. He became a rapist because his owner didn't look after him well enough, he didn't train him the right way. The rapist was not conditioned the way in which other people were. Gradually, over time, a man can become a rapist. I hate rapists, you know that, but I have to be open-minded enough to accept that it is perhaps not the rapist's fault. – I have to accept that it's certainly not entirely his fault that he became what he became; it has also something to do with his owner.

The problem is, I can't talk to the rapist's owner and negotiate some sort of arrangement that ensures that the rapist never again does what he did. The owner who could fix the problem is untraceable: invisible. I can't phone him, write a letter to him or send him an email, not even an SMS. He's left the building and left no forwarding address. So what options do I have? Let's be fair about this. If I want to be certain that a brutal rapist – one that's outside the reach of the law – cannot rape another woman ever again, I have to do something that prevents him from doing it ever again. And that's what Ella and I did without feelings of hate, pleasure, or guilt. Only with the certain knowledge that the men we were dealing with could never repeat their crimes.

Apart from doing to rapists what we did, we were good people. What we did was bad according to the law; it was a crime. However, my assessment you probably know by now, someone's got to do it.

I do accept the reality of the situation. Legally, Ella and I are criminals, although, in our opinion, we simply did a job that someone needed to do.

Ella and I stopped punishing rapists together about six months before we separated. At that time, I received a phone call from one of my Tough Contacts. We chatted for a while about this and that, and in the process, she mentioned (the contact was an elderly woman) that a fourteen-year-old girl in the neighborhood had been brutally raped. She also told me the name of the perpetrator, a twenty-three-year-old man who lived in the neighborhood. I mentioned what my TC had told me to Ella. She looked at me with a sullen look in her eyes. Somehow, I understood what that meant. No more. It was okay with me.

But then, a few days later, I decided that I had to do something about it after all. You can't just stop hating what you hate most. This time, I did something different. Half of the man's penis ended up in a rubbish bin in a park nearby. This was the first time, blood was spilled. Later, I learned when the girl he had raped heard about it, she was relieved.

During the months that followed, I added a few more men with shortened penises to that part of New York.

I realize I haven't told you what punishment *exactly* Ella and I dished out to the really bad guys. Let me think about it. Maybe I'll tell you later. Let me see how I feel about it as things progress.

3

Back to the old lady and me in the car, which used to belong to the dead man in the crosswalk who by now was several miles behind us. I was hoping other cars didn't run over him as the truck had done, although it wouldn't have done him any further harm. It would have been a damn mess and made life difficult for the ambulance people, though.

"What proposition?" I asked.

"Before we talk about that," the old lady replied, "we should get rid of this car."

That was a perfectly logical thought which should have occurred to me. But it hadn't. What kind of old lady was there sitting beside me?

"Have you done this kind of thing before?" I asked.

"No… not really…" she said. It didn't sound convincing.

"You aren't telling me the truth."

"It is the truth!" she emphasized. "I've seen it on TV."

"What have you seen on TV?"

"How to get rid of a car."

"That's the easy part," I said. "We park it somewhere and walk away."

"What about our finger prints?" she asked.

Again! I couldn't help wondering: what kind of old lady was there sitting beside me?

"We park the car as you said," I could hear her say, "and we walk away as you said. But before we walk away, we start a little fire."

And that was exactly what we did. We stopped in a quiet street. She gave me her scarf and told me to hang it in the opening of the gas tank. "Let the scarf go down as far as possible," she said. "It has to be saturated with gas. Let's hope the tank is reasonably full."

What a lady! I did exactly as instructed. She told me to make sure there was a bit of gas on the upholstery of the seats. "Just squeeze a bit of gas out of the scarf," she said. Then she suggested that I place the scarf underneath the driver's seat and light it with a match, of which she coincidentally had a box in her pocket. "But don't forget to open the windows first," she pointed out. "A good fire needs oxygen."

She would walk away first, she said, because she was getting on a bit and wasn't as fast on her feet as she used to be. I should wait five minutes, then start the fire under the driver's seat and follow her. It would take a minute or two before the fire would engulf the inside of the car and be noticed, that should give me enough time to catch up with her. We would take a taxi and go to her place. We would switch taxis several times so that it would be as good as impossible for the police to discover the location of her place with the help of the taxi drivers.

And that was what we did. My elderly companion was extraordinarily cautious. The last taxi we used, she asked to stop a few hundred yards before we reached her apartment. She paid the driver, and we walked the remaining distance.

What a lady!

4

She lived in an expensive apartment building in an upscale part of Manhattan. There was an athletic-looking man who let us into the building. He glanced at me suspiciously, but he knew Irene Sonntag, and after they had exchanged a few pleasantries, the old lady and I found ourselves in a lift up to the top floor.

Her apartment was a surprise. It was big, had many rooms, and magnificent views over Manhattan, as you would expect from a top floor location. But that wasn't the only surprise. The furniture, the artwork, the colors, in fact, the entire atmosphere of the place didn't look at all like what you would expect from a place of that kind that belongs to a lady in her nineties. It looked like the place of someone much younger. Everything was modern, elegant, and extraordinarily tasteful and harmonious.

"Who else lives here?" I asked

"Only me and you," she replied.

Me and *you?*

"I didn't know that I was living here."

"That's my proposal," the old lady continued. "I am inviting you to live with me. You will have your own quarters: a living room, bedroom, study, and bath of course. Apart from that, you can use the entire apartment as if it were your own. There are lots of rooms, a library, gym, a music room, TV room, and a big kitchen of course. Have a look around. Take your time."

I had a look around. I took my time.

"Why do you want me to live with you?"

"You are a writer," she said.

"How do you know?" I was surprised. I hadn't told her anything yet about myself except my name and age.

"I've read your books. Some time ago, I looked you up on the Internet and saw your picture on Amazon. I recognized you straight away when you came to help me in the crosswalk."

"Ok. I'm a writer. But that doesn't explain why you want me to move in to your apartment."

"Have you seen the library?"

She was not answering my question. She always found something else to talk about.

"Yes," I answered, "I have seen the library. She's huge. I hope you don't mind if I call your library a *she*."

"That seems appropriate."

"How many books do you have in there?"

She looked at me for a minute as if she had to first discuss her answer with herself. Then she caught a deep breath and said, "There are exactly 8,640 books. But the books are not the problem. There are active literary characters in that library. They are harder to handle. I'm not sure how many exactly, but by my last estimate I would say about 150 to 200, although some of them have not been active for a while; I'm not sure if they are still around or what happened to them."

"Interesting. Very interesting. Would you mind telling me a bit more about these literary characters?"

She looked at me suspiciously before she asked, "You don't think I should see a psychologist?"

"No, no! Not at all. I'm familiar with literary characters. A psychologist wouldn't necessarily know what to do with them."

"Last night Pursewarden was here."

"Ah! – I've read about him. He can be unpredictable."

"Unpredictable, arrogant, entertaining, but also very generous," she added.

"Complex, I guess, is the word."

At that moment, Pursewarden entered the room.

"Talk about the devil…" Irene said but didn't finish the sentence.

"Is that him?" I asked.

"That's him."

"I've met you in my imaginary world," I said to the man who'd just entered the room, "but I didn't know you also existed in real life."

"What do you know about real life?" He sounded a tad arrogant, just the way Lawrence Durrell had created him.

"Maybe not a lot," I replied, "but I have no reason to doubt that this here, this conversation, is taking place in what I call *my real life*."

"If you say so."

"I do say so. But tell me, why are you terrorizing this old lady?"

Before Pursewarden could reply, the old lady jumped to his defence. "He is not really terrorizing me. He is quite a good boy."

"Oh," I couldn't help repeating with a bit of mockery, "You are quite a good boy. Did you hear that? That's interesting."

"I am the way Lawrence wants me to be."

"Good point," I had to admit, "but Lawrence is dead."

"What do you know about death?" He didn't mean it as a question, more as a statement. I said nothing, which was not an easy thing for me to do. As you know, I am a writer and used to be a professional speaker. I can always think of something to say. But this time, I had to agree with Pursewarden, whose statement implied that I knew nothing about death. He was right I knew practically nothing about death.

Pursewarden said, "I'll be back later," and left the room towards the library.

5

You may not have heard of Pursewarden unless you've read Lawrence Durrell's *Alexandria Quartet*, which comprises the four novels *Justine, Balthazar, Mountolive* and *Clea*. Durrell wrote these books between 1957 and 1962 when according to my calculation, the old lady would have been in her mid to late thirties.

Now, more than five decades later, she told me she had read each of these four books, five times.

"Usually, I don't read fiction books that often," she said. "Maybe I read a novel twice if the book is outstanding, but of the thousands of novels I've read, there are about a dozen I've read three and four times and some five times."

"Are the characters from these novels the ones that now intrude into your life?" I asked.

"Not all of them, but some," she replied.

At this point, a few words about Durrell's *Alexandria Quartet*, to give you an idea about Pursewarden and the people, time, and places where he lived.

Where he lived? For heaven's sake, what's the matter with me? He is a fictional character… Why do I talk about him as if he were a historical figure?

Maybe Pursewarden had a point after all when he challenged me and asked: "What do you know about real life?"

The narrator of Lawrence Durrell's *Alexandria Quartet* is a fictional writer by the name of L. G. Darley. (I suspect Lawrence modelled Darley on himself.) Darley is still young and has a mistress, Melissa. They don't truly love each other, but that's another story. Somehow, with Melissa's help, Darley becomes Justine's lover. She is Jewish and the wife of a rich businessman. A young and beautiful artist, *Clea*, also has an affair with Darley. But Darley is crazy about Justine, who's a rather complex person. As a girl, she was raped by a man named Capodistria. This, it is said, is the reason for her being a sex-addict.

Most of the events described in *The Alexandria Quartet* took place just before World War II.

Darley thinks Justine's husband intends to murder him at a duck-shooting party. After all, he had sex with the man's wife. But instead, apparently by accident, the man who had raped Justine years earlier is shot. (I don't have to tell you how that pleased me.) Justine leaves her husband and moves to a kibbutz in Palestine.

Pursewarden is a well-established novelist. He is a somewhat arrogant and cynical character, but with lots of charisma. He doesn't appear all that often in the four books, but when he appears, he always says or does something that makes you remember him. When he applied for a passport and was questioned about his religion, he wrote that he is a Protestant, but only in the sense that he protests. Darley doesn't like Pursewarden, but that doesn't prevent him from admiring the man.

Darley goes away for a couple of years. When he returns to Alexandria to see Melissa, who is very ill, he finds he is too late. Melissa is dead. She had a child from a character called Nessim. Darley, the good man he is (a bit like Durrell himself?), decides to look after the child. They move to a Greek island where Darryl writes the story.

Now we learn what really has been going on. Justine didn't truly love Darley either. She was in love with Pursewarden. But at one time, Pursewarden had kicked her out of his hotel room. Then, the marriage between Justine and her rich husband wasn't all that great, but the sex between the two of them was good.

Darley and Pursewarden turn out to be British spies. (I bet you didn't see that coming.)

Then there is the British Ambassador – Mountolive – and an intense political conspiracy. Remember, these events took place just before and at the beginning of the Second World War. Someone gets assassinated. There are a few bad men… One of them, Mountolive, had an affair with a beautiful woman; later, when she had lost all her beauty, she asked him to protect her son, but he rejected her pitilessly.

But there is revenge, as there usually is. Somehow, Mountolive ends up visiting a brothel. I believe it might have been Justine who had lured him there. He becomes the lover of Pursewarden's blind sister. Mountolive and Pursewarden's sister marry, why I do not recall. Mountolive ended up looking like a fool.

Then Pursewarden, it seems, had enough of all the hullabaloo and committed suicide. What happens next? Darley and Pursewarden's sister burn Pursewarden's collection of letters, which is a bit of a shame. Apparently, his letters were a lot better than his novels, which weren't exactly bad either.

There is more about Clea and there is also Balthazar, who I haven't mentioned so far. There is drama under water when Darley has to amputate someone's hand. I'll leave it at that. What I wanted to say about Pursewarden I have said. He is the true artist. I think it was him who said – or was it Darley? You may like to check that should you ever read the books: *"There is not enough faith, charity, or tenderness to furnish this world with a single ray of hope – yet so long as that strange, sad cry rings out over the world, the birth-pangs of an artist – all cannot be lost!"*

6

"How about a glass of wine?" the old Lady asked.

"I need something stronger," I replied. "One doesn't meet Pursewarden every day. How about a whiskey, double, and without ice?"

The old Lady went to a cabinet and returned with a magnificent bottle of George Dickel Tennessee that, from the looks of it, must have been a century old.

"You have seen where the bottle's coming from," she said, "whiskey glasses are over there. You are invited to make this place your home, so please help yourself."

I went to the vitrine she had pointed to and took two whiskey glasses and showed them to her. She nodded. I half-filled both glasses and handed one to her and kept the other one for myself. The whiskey was of a quality and depth of flavor beyond words.

"It started about six months ago," Irene continued, "when one evening at around nine o'clock a man walked in here and said, 'Please don't be alarmed, I am not an intruder. I am a literary character from one of the books in your library.'"

"Were you alarmed?"

"Strangely enough, I wasn't. I said to that character, 'And who may I ask are you?' He replied, 'I'm Jay Gatsby, generally known as the Great Gatsby.'"

"What did he look like?"

"He looked handsome and rich."

"And then?"

"And then… I don't know what got into me. I said to him, 'I've never heard of you. Which book are you from?'"

"Wow!" I couldn't help but laugh.

"The gentleman didn't think that was funny. He looked rather shocked and said, 'But you must remember me. You've read the book. I do remember you, so you must remember me!' He wasn't as cool as I thought the Great Gatsby would be, and his sense of humor was rather underdeveloped."

"Are you pulling my leg?"

"No. Definitely not. The man was shocked; he dropped onto the sofa exactly at the same spot where you are sitting now. I asked him if I could offer him a glass of water or coffee. 'A glass of water would be appreciated', he said, and I fetched him a glass of water. As he drank I said to him, 'Look, of course I've read *The Great Gatsby* and know you from the book, I'm just having a bit of fun because it's obvious that I am dreaming.' You should have seen how relieved he was."

"I wish I'd had been there," I said

"You'll get to know him, don't worry."

"What did he want?"

"I'll tell you in a minute. After I told him that I must have been dreaming, he made every effort to convince me that I wasn't. 'Everything is real,' he insisted. 'Oh yeah,' I retorted, 'you are Jay Gatsby and I am Daisy Buchanan'. You remember Daisy, don't you? The girl, well, Tom Buchanan's wife, really, with whom Gatsby was in love."

"Oh yes, I remember her," I said.

"We argued about whether or not I was dreaming. It went on like that for a while until I said to him, 'Look, I'm tired. It's time for me to go to bed. What is it that you want?' Please prepare yourself for a surprise. What do you think was his answer?"

"I've no idea."

"I am not happy with the ending," she replied.

7

For days, I had been tossing up whether or not I should talk to Irene Sonntag about my past. The punishing of rapists, the recent penis amputations, that kind of stuff. I was wondering what you, the reader, would have done? I guess some of you would say, 'tell her'. Some of you would say, 'don't tell her'.

You are not a great help.

I had a theory that could explain how it was possible for literary characters to appear in real life. This is an interesting topic: both from a philosophical perspective, and in recent years, also from the perspective of theoretical physics.

I was wondering if I should discuss this topic with some of the literary characters in Irene's apartment.

I used to receive a call about twice a week on my cell phone from my TCs. Most of the time, they told me the latest about unreported crimes. Sometimes, they asked for advice, and sometimes they surprised me with pieces of good news. In case you are wondering if I was ever worried that these calls could be traced by the police – no, I wasn't. Calls to my cell phone could not be traced. A friend of mine who worked in the IT Department of the Telco provider to whom my cell phone was connected, had written a little program that he had hidden amongst thousands of other Telco programs. This particular program ensured that every trace of every call to and from my phone was erased immediately after the completion of the call.

The old lady told me that she was ninety-two when I met her.

8

"What did he mean?" I asked. "He was not happy with the ending?"

"Do you remember the ending?"

"Gatsby was floating dead in the swimming pool. Shot, I believe."

"That's what he doesn't like," the old lady pointed out.

"Really!" I couldn't believe it, almost yelling. "That's none of his business! That's the author's business. Fitzgerald decided that he had to die, he decided how he had to die, and that's it. Gatsby just has to accept it. Don't you think so?"

Irene didn't quite agree with me. "From a literary perspective," she said, "you have a valid point. But what's the scenario like if you look at it from Gatsby's perspective? He was killed and nobody had asked him if this was okay with him. And then, don't forget, there might also be a legal perspective?"

"A legal perspective?"

"Yes. What prevents Gatsby today from taking the matter to court?"

"Ha, that would be a hell of a spectacle."

"That's an understatement. It would be the spectacle of the century. But Gatsby told me he has no intention of doing that. Not at this stage."

"Not at this stage?"

"No, not at this stage," Irene confirmed.

I couldn't believe I was having this conversation. "In any case, who would he take to court?" I asked. "F. Scott Fitzgerald is dead."

"Perhaps the current publisher of the book," the old lady replied.

"Is this what he said?"

"No, no. I'm speculating. In the first instance, he wants something entirely different."

"What does he want?"

"He wants the ending of the book to be rewritten."

9

Jay Gatsby wanted the ending of the book that has his name in the title, to be rewritten. Pursewarden, who had committed suicide, asked for that part of the book that deals with his death to be rewritten. "No suicide for me," he said. The aging fisherman, Santiago from *The Old Man and the Sea* felt very strongly about the need to have the book edited; not only did he want to return from his fishing ordeal with his marlin intact, he also wanted to bring the shark home. And then there was Lady Brett Ashley from Hemingway's novel *Fiesta*, which was originally published as *The Sun Also Rises*. Lady Ashley was adamant that major parts of the book had to be rewritten. For decades, she said, she had suffered devastatingly because of Jake's impotence. How Hemingway could do such a thing to her and Jake was beyond her comprehension. Then, there was a character from

John Irving's *The World According to Garp*. I've forgotten his name but felt sorry for him. He had his penis bitten off by Garp's wife who was giving him a blow job when Garp's car crashed into his car. He wanted that scene deleted from the book, and I thought he had a point. Mona, the most important character in Henry Miller's books after Henry Miller himself, had comparatively modest demands. She asked for the truth. When Irene told her that she was a fictional character and the truth was whatever the author wrote about her, she strongly disagreed. Her real name – she insisted – was June, and she was Henry's real wife from 1924 to 1934, and accordingly, she wanted the name Mona to be changed to June. Some of Henry's exaggerations she wanted to see corrected, and other bits and pieces, which Henry neglected to include, she wanted to have included. Thinking about it, I was probably wrong when I thought at first that this was a modest demand. A criminal from an Edgar Wallace novel turned up and talked about a trial in which he felt he was misrepresented. He didn't look like a criminal and asked politely if this matter could please be rectified. Could it be, I wondered, that Edgar had made a mistake? Walter Faber and his daughter, Sabeth, appeared together and without having to ask them I knew what they wanted. Walter and Sabeth were lovers before he discovered that she was his daughter. Yes, I felt for them. *Homo Faber* by Max Frisch was a book that would have to be totally rewritten if it was meant to satisfy these two characters. Josef Bloch, a literary character from Peter Handke's Roman *Die Angst des Tormanns beim Elfmeter*, suggested that the last paragraph of the book should be rewritten. That's all. Nothing else. He was happy for the goalkeeper to get hold of the ball (he had been a goalkeeper once himself), but it would have been better if the *Elfmeterschütze* had kicked the ball towards the upper right-hand corner of the goal and not straight into the goalkeeper's hands. I didn't dispute this point. Alexei Ivanovich from Fyodor Dostoyevsky's *The Gambler* was all in all happy with the way the famous author had portrayed him, only the ending with his love Polina in Switzerland, he thought, was a bit harsh. Then, there was a bit of a surprise when Philip Carey *Of Human Bondage* turned up. "You can't be serious. You have nothing to complain," Irene said to him.

"I agree," he replied, "I'm alright."

"So what do you want?"

"I just want it to be known," he said, "that I think that all my literary character colleagues should return to where they came from and accept that life is what it is."

Iris from Margaret Atwood's *The Blind Assassin* was present when Philip Carey expressed his opinion. She said to him, "You have no idea what the fuck you are talking about. You have to have lived life on four levels concurrently before you know what life is all about."

"Four levels? Are you sure?" the old lady asked surprised.

"Whatever!" Iris replied. She was in a bad mood and didn't sound like a character from the 1940s.

It went on like this for nearly two months. Usually, one or two literary characters turned up every evening. Some didn't stay long, maybe only ten minutes, then Irene and I had the rest of the evening for ourselves. Some did accept the old lady's invitation for dinner, though, and stayed until midnight. At times, the characters seemed a bit unreasonable, while others presented their cases convincingly, and it was a pleasure to listen to their reasoning. Jay Gatsby and Pursewarden turned up several times. When we invited Pursewarden for dinner, he replied that fictional characters don't eat, but he wouldn't mind a cognac. (Later, as I got to know him better, he changed his view about eating). He stayed until after midnight and the two of us finished an entire bottle of Rémy Martin Louis XIII. "The king of cognacs," Pursewarden commented approvingly. Irene sipped from my glass and switched back to her Penfolds Grange.

The last character that arrived was Jesus. He had to introduce himself just as so many others before him. We would not have recognized him. The color of his skin wasn't white, his hair wasn't long, and he just didn't look at all like the man I had seen on hundreds of pictures since my childhood. Irene was also surprised and asked him if he was sure he wasn't an imposter.

"Heck, no!" he laughed. "I'm truly Jesus."

We asked him why he was here. After all, Irene pointed out, he wasn't meant to be a fictional character. He was both, he replied, fictional and real.

Irene interpreted this as meaning that over the centuries, quite a bit about him had been twisted and misrepresented and today it was hard, or even impossible, to separate fact from fiction.

But he said that wasn't what he meant.

"You lost me," I said.

"Ah!" he replied, "that's a good point. The fictional Jesus is allowed to lose you, but the real one will never lose you."

"*Never ever?*" I asked.

"*Never ever!*" he confirmed. "No matter what you do, no matter where you go, He won't lose you."

I thought about this for a moment before I asked, "What if I became an atheist, a Buddhist, or converted to Islam?"

Without hesitating, he answered, "Wouldn't make the slightest difference."

Very interesting, I thought.

The old lady asked, "What can we do for you?"

He replied, "You could arrange for someone to rewrite the fictional Jesus. Polish him up a bit. Make him more interesting. Perhaps inject a bit of humor and give him a sexy girlfriend."

"Are you talking about the *Holy Book*?"

"Not really, I am talking about *The Bible*."

"But not everything in *The Bible* is fiction?"

"It's a mixture of fiction, riddles, wisdom, history, bemusing sentences, strange grammar, and lots of incorrect translations."

"And what do you want us to do?" I asked as if I had not understood what he had said a few seconds earlier.

"Rewrite the book in plain English. Make it sound like a good Hemingway or Salinger novel, but a bit more humorous please. Maybe throw a bit of Kishon in."

"Who is Kishon?"

"He is a Jew, but you can't blame him for that. He's a good man and can be very funny."

"But why do you want to have the biggest bestseller of all times rewritten?" I asked.

"I want people to read the book!" he answered emphatically. "Today, millions of people have a copy of the Bible, but how many have read it?"

"How many?"

"Not many."

10

The media reported that the police were looking for an old woman and an old man, who together had caused the death of a young man and stolen and later destroyed his car.

They showed pictures of what looked indeed like two old people. Irene looked just like tens of thousands of old women in New York, and I looked like an old man, but only because I was wearing an old jacket and an old and scrappy farmer's hat. My face was covered by shade and unrecognizable. I had received the hat as a gift from an Australian farmer nearly ten years earlier at the end of the harvesting season. I was on a trip around the world and worked for the farmer to improve my travel budget.

(I was also in love with the man's daughter, but that's a story for another day.) Some people had used their cell phones and iPhones to take pictures and videos of what had happened. But all recordings were made after the young man had been hit by the truck. Nobody had bothered to record what had taken place before. And fortunately, probably because of all the noise and traffic that was going on, the pictures and recordings were of sufficiently below average quality. Neither Irene nor I were overly worried about being recognized.

Just to be on the safe side, though, we got rid of what we were wearing when we met the first time in that crosswalk. When I burned my hat, I felt sad and said to him, "Sorry mate, you served me well, and I bear you no ill will, but circumstances beyond my control force me to permanently distance myself from you." I think he understood. And yes, a man's hat is a *he*.

11

There was one evening when I asked Jean-Baptiste Adamsberg what he thought was the reason that so many literary characters in Irene's library had decided to leave their books and mix with real people. "You are one of them," I said. "What made you decide to leave the fictional world created by Fred Vargas and turn up here, in the real world?"

He looked at me and said that he didn't know there were two different worlds. To him, there has always been one world only. He then asked what it was that made me think that my so-called real world was different from his so-called fictional world. He added, "The properties are the same."

I had forgotten that he was into Zen. Nevertheless… "The properties! What are the properties?" I asked and probably looked a bit dumbfounded.

"Well, the stuff which the entire world is made of."

"What is the world made of?"

"Stuff," he said.

"What stuff?"

"Stuff made of stuff."

"You're pulling my leg."

"Not really."

"That stuff that you are referring to, does it have a name?" I asked. For a policeman, he wasn't very specific.

"The name of the stuff is stuff."

"The word stuff is a generic expression," I argued and probably felt a bit like his colleague Adrien Danglard at times. "The word stuff is about as non-specific as a word can be, and accordingly, it can mean just about anything: steel, stone, timber, gas, even dreams can be referred to as stuff."

"That's it! It's all made of the same stuff. Steel, stone, timber, gas, even dreams are all made of exactly the same stuff."

"And what is this stuff? But now, please don't tell me it's stuff."

"But that's exactly what it is. There is nothing else. When Fred Vargas created me, she created me out of stuff. By the way, you know her real name is Frédérique Audoin-Rouzeau?"

"I know." I didn't want him to change the topic.

"And so I am stuff," he continued. "She, too, is stuff. When you write a novel, you create stuff out of stuff. You are stuff and your creations are stuff. When an architect designs a building, he designs stuff out of stuff and when other people later build the building, they, too, make it out of stuff and the building is stuff. There really isn't anything else, as far as I can see. Some stuff is called steel, some is called a car, a house, a city, a book, a story, some of it is called the plot of a novel, love, hate, surprise, emotions, mountains, planets, the universe… You know what I mean; I could go on and on; it's all stuff made exactly of the same stuff."

"Can you describe the physical properties of the stuff you are talking about?" I asked.

"Nobody can," he replied. "You can't describe stuff with stuff. There is a limit as to how far you can go. You can create stuff with stuff, but you can't explain stuff with stuff. Or in other words, there comes a point where you have to accept reality."

"So what's reality? No, don't tell me. I think I know your answer. *Stuff.*"

"Good. You got it."

"No. I am becoming sarcastic."

"Oh! Sarcasm's also stuff."

"You know he had a point," said Irene to me after Jean-Baptiste Adamsberg had left. All the time while he and I were talking about stuff, she was enjoying a glass of wine and listening without interrupting us.

"I know," I said. "He has a point, a very valid point."

"It's the same point that some people think Jesus made two-thousand years ago. We should ask him about it the next time he turns up."

"True, very true," I agreed. "Even our physicists are catching up and arriving at the same point. There is only subatomic particle stuff, Higgs boson stuff, God particle stuff, thought stuff, call it what you like."

"So what's the problem?"

"The problem is, there has never been such a thing called 'two thousand years ago'. There has been no Jesus two thousand years ago. There is no time, never has been. There is only stuff. This Tennessee Whiskey is stuff. My thoughts are stuff. My imaginations are stuff. Eternity is stuff. I can live with this, but…"

"But?"

"Where the heck did stuff originate from?"

The old lady was smart enough not to attempt to answer that question. At this stage, we both knew there would have been only one five-letter answer possible.

Stuff.

12

I had been living with the old lady for several months when I returned to my question: Why did she want me to move in with her? A question which Irene still hadn't answered, probably because at the time when I asked initially our conversation was interrupted by Pursewarden. In the meantime, I had moved into her apartment and we had a hell of a great time with her daily visitors from the library, and my question had been pushed to the background. But now, I asked her again.

"That was a spontaneous decision," she explained. "I like your books; my favourite one is your novel about the banker, his wife and the two bohemians. Then, when you came to my assistance and I recognized you – and then even more so when you willingly drove away with me from the accident scene in the dead man's car – that was the moment when the thought occurred to me that you could be just the right man to help me with the literary characters in my home. By the way, why did you so easily agree with my suggestion to take the dead man's car and drive away?"

"You didn't just suggest it. You made me do it."

"Not in a legal sense."

"No, but perhaps you hypnotized me."

"Seriously, why did you so quickly agree with my suggestion to take the dead man's car and drive away?"

"Good question," I replied. "I think I was simply bored with my life, and what you suggested seemed to be a kind of unpredictably exciting thing to do. It really was a fascinating suggestion."

"You don't get flustered easily."

I didn't reply, and I don't think Irene expected a reply. But she was right, and I hope this doesn't sound conceited. I don't get ruffled easily. Early on in my life, I learned that it is a good thing to live without great expectations. Or maybe I should say without specific expectations. I don't mean this in a negative way, and I certainly don't mean one should not have goals or ambitions. I have great goals and I am ambitious, but I don't have this perfectionist mentality that I have to achieve my goals or that my ambitions are particularly important. Goals and ambitions are useful to provide one's life with a sense of purpose and direction, but beyond that, they mean little. They definitely are not meant to result in stress, which of course is exactly what can easily happen if they are combined with strong expectations. In this regard, my reality is straightforward: goals and ambitions can be put aside from one moment to the next, or one can let them hibernate for a while, or even discard them all together and come up with new ones.

When Irene asked me to drive away with her in the dead man's car, I remember quite clearly the kind of thinking that flashed through my mind. You may recall, she walked unexpectedly to the car and entered it through the passenger door. I entered the car at the driver's side, and she said, "Let's go." I was surprised and repeated what she said, but in a questioning tone: "Let's go?!" And Irene said, "You can drive a car, can't you? Let's get away from here. What are you waiting for?" Then, looking at her, I realized within the fraction of a second three features about her:

she was quite old, she had sparkling eyes, and she displayed a charismatic beauty. I am sure I arrived at these impressions in less than a second. Then, maybe within a second or two, my mind addressed her suggestion to go, to drive away, and went something like: *that's crazy, that's illegal; but an interesting idea; something different; what's the worst that can happen? Trouble with the police, maybe a fine; I can live with that. Let's do it.*

I put the car into first gear, released the clutch, made sure I didn't drive over the dead body, and a few seconds later, when we found ourselves in the middle of the crossing, I realized that cars were heading towards us on the left and right, so I pushed the accelerator pedal down as fast and hard as I could. And I may add, I was quite impressed by how well that old Ford responded.

"Interesting," I said, continuing my conversation with the old lady. "After I had spontaneously agreed to steal a car and leave the scene of a hit and run in the company of a strange elderly lady, you had decided spontaneously that it might be a good idea to invite me to move in with you. Is that how things happened?"

"I think that pretty much sums it up."

"I just wish everything in life were that easy."

"Well, I guess things are always as easy or as difficult as we make them, and in this instance, we both had the good sense to make quick and easy decisions."

13

"You look like a pastor," said Irene to the man who had just entered the room. He was a man in his early forties, give or take a few years, and the only unusual thing about him was the direction from which he had entered the room. So far, all literary characters had come from the direction of the library, but this character – and I assumed that he was one of them – had come from the direction of that part of the apartment where my quarters were located.

"I'm a pastor, and I was created by a pastor," the man replied.

"Ha! Created by Tom Hilpert!?" I exclaimed.

"Yes, he is my immediate creator; my true creator of course is a bit higher up the echelon."

"That's a great way of putting it," Irene commented.

"So you must be the crime-fighting pastor Jonah Borden from Tom Hilpert's novel *Superior Justice*," I stated. At the same moment, a thought occurred to me which at first I found somewhat irritating.

"Yes, that's me, coming directly from the Lake Superior area," the man replied.

"You didn't emerge from the library area?" I asked.

"No," he replied, "I've heard of libraries but never seen one."

"You have never seen a room full of books?" Irene asked.

"No."

"You came from my room, and in my room, you jumped out of my Kindle, correct?" I asked.

"That's correct, except I didn't jump."

"How did you do it? I mean how did you manage to convert yourself from millions of pixels into a man of flesh, blood and skin?"

"I walked out."

"You walked out of my Kindle?"

"That's correct."

"Is there any point in me trying to further explore this topic?"

"To be honest," the pastor who had walked out from my eBook replied, "there is probably no point. I doubt that I could explain it adequately."

"You don't know?"

"I don't have a clue. It just happened."

"What can we do for you?" the old lady inquired.

"I would like to ask Jesus a few questions. In the digital book world where I come from, there is a rumor going around."

There is a rumor going around in the digital book world? I didn't trust my ears.

"What rumor?" Irene asked.

"Are you saying in the digital book world there is communication going on between literary characters?" I asked.

"Which question do you want me to address first?" the pastor asked.

"Tell us about the rumor first," I replied.

"I met Pursewarden a few days ago, and he told me about this apartment and the things that are happening here. He also mentioned that, as far as he was aware, Jesus was here."

"Yes, he was here for a few hours," Irene confirmed, "but whether or not we can arrange a meeting between you and him, I don't know. I don't think we can just go into the library and summon him."

"You could try."

"Yeah," I agreed, "we could try. So far our meetings with literary characters have been a one-way street. They just turn up. Maybe we can go to the library and ask one or the other to visit us."

"Could we start with Jesus?" the pastor suggested.

All three of us ventured into the library. The pastor who had never been in a library before had a good look around before he said that the place pretty much looked the way he had anticipated it. "Lots of paper," he added. "In the world where I come from, you could store all these books on a little chip the size of a fingernail."

"But you couldn't smell them," Irene commented.

"Good point," the pastor replied. Then, after a few seconds, he asked, "Why would you like to smell them?"

"That's also a good point," the old lady replied. "But don't worry about it, I don't think I could explain it to you."

After a few seconds Irene said, "Hello!" She spoke loud and clear. "We have a visitor here for Jesus. Jesus, could you please come and see him?"

We discussed whether we should wait in the library for Jesus to appear or return to the living room. We decided to wait for a few minutes in the library, but after Jesus hadn't miraculously slipped out of the Bible nor anybody else had appeared, we returned to the living room.

I opened a bottle of wine and asked the pastor if he expected to become the protagonist of another novel. He told me that this had already happened and mentioned the title of the book. "Great," I said, "that could well be my next read. Is the book available as an eBook?" He said it was, and we went to my computer and to Amazon.com, and a few minutes later the book had found its way into my Kindle. Then, a thought occurred to me.

"This doesn't make sense," I said. "How can you be here and in the book at the same time?"

"Good question."

I opened the book in my Kindle and started to page through it and discovered that wherever the pastor should have appeared in the text there was a comment saying: 'Pastor Jonah Borden is temporarily unavailable'.

"My goodness!" Irene yelled half serious, half laughing. "Just think of all the poor people who are reading the book right now and are told that the most important character of the story is temporarily unavailable."

"Damn!" the pastor said. "What a shit!"

"Damn? What a shit? You are a man of the cloth, how can you say that?" Irene asked.

"Cloth or not, what would you have said?"

"Damn! What a shit! I would have said."

I could see that everybody felt like laughing but wasn't entirely certain if this was the appropriate thing to do. I filled three glasses of wine and said, "Cheers!"

The young woman was beautiful; perhaps not so much in a classical sense, but definitely in a charismatic sense. By that I mean, she didn't just look like a stunning piece of art, there was more to her; she looked more like an interesting piece of art. You didn't just want to have sex with her, you felt more like looking at her, turning her around and exploring her, and then make love to her. She arrived from the direction of the library and said, "I hope I'm not intruding."

"Please join us," Irene said.

I fetched another glass, filled it with wine, gave it to her and said, "Prost!"

"Skål!" she replied and granted me the most gorgeous smile I had ever seen in my life.

"I don't believe we've met before. What can we do for you?" Irene asked.

"I'm Lisbeth Salander," the woman said. "I'm here on behalf of Jesus. He told me one of you would like to meet him, but he can't make it today, so he asked me to represent him."

"Represent him?" Jonah Borden, the literary pastor asked disbelievingly. "He's God. Nobody can represent God."

"Oh no!" the gorgeous woman laughed. "Firstly, we are talking here about the literary Jesus. Secondly and more importantly, *everybody* can represent God."

"*Everybody?*"

"Of course! God is everybody and everything, and accordingly, everybody and everything do represent God."

"All the time?"

"Yes, all the time."

"I see."

"So, why did you want to meet Jesus?"

"I wanted to ask him a question," the literary pastor replied.

"Please ask."

"There is no need anymore. I wanted to ask him: who or what is God? You've just answered it. Thank you. "

"You're welcome."

"Are you sure that's the correct and complete answer and there is nothing else to it?" the old lady asked.

"As far as this existence is concerned, that's it!" Lisbeth Salander replied with a smile.

"So there could be more to it in another existence?"

"As far as we are concerned, everything outside of this existence is beyond us."

PART 2: Love, sex and legal complications

14

"There is no point denying it," the old lady said to me the next day, "you're in love with a famous literary character."

"I'm attracted to her, that's for sure."

Things were getting complicated.

Lisbeth Salander had stayed for several hours. The four of us, Irene, Lisbeth, the pastor, and I had dinner together with several bottles of red wine. By eleven, I was drunk and could see the same was the case with Irene. Lisbeth and the pastor, both of whom had consumed about twice as much wine as I, seemed to handle their alcohol all right. They hardly showed signs of intoxication.

"You alright?" Lisbeth asked me.

"Never felt better," I replied and was wondering whether my voice sounded slurred or if I still had that part of my persona sufficiently under control. "Just need to get a handkerchief," I said and got up. The truth was I wanted to take two aspirin tablets in the privacy of my quarters.

Lisbeth got up with me and said, "I need a handkerchief too." Nobody said a word, and Lisbeth followed me into my room.

"Don't you feel stoned?" I asked her. "You had a lot more of that wine than I."

"Literary characters don't get stoned that easily," she replied. "But hell, it's a nice wine."

"About two hundred dollars a bottle," I said.

"Usually I don't drink wine."

"What does one drink in the literary world?" I asked.

Lisbeth didn't answer my question. She went to the sofa and undressed. I stood and watched her. She was even more beautiful than I remembered her from reading Stieg Larsson's books. I no longer felt the alcohol in my head. I looked at her and smiled, a bit like the way one would look at a delicious dessert about to be consumed, but without being in a hurry.

I undressed as well. She watched me with the same calm look in her eyes.

We lay on the sofa and kissed and snuggled together, and when I had a nipple of her firm breasts between my teeth, she whispered, "No need for a long foreplay, I am ready."

So was I, but in no hurry. I entered her and moved slowly. I loved to rub my chest against her breasts and leisurely stirred in and out of her, feeling the increasing heat inside her and myself. Her orgasm came quickly, and her slim and tender body shook as if it had come in contact with an electric power line. "Now slow down," she said. "Just stop. Stay inside me, but don't move." I did as she said. A few minutes later, I felt her moving and heard her say, "Now let's go for it, hard and fast. The second time it takes a bit longer with me, and we may be able to come together."

She was right. We had sex, we made love, we showed passion, and tortured ourselves as if there was no tomorrow. And who knows, maybe there wasn't going to be a tomorrow for a woman and a man like her and me: creatures from different worlds. But I didn't think about that; this thought occurred to me later, and I'm sure she didn't think about this complexity either.

Our orgasms exploded within seconds of each other, and we stayed on the sofa for another thirty minutes before we returned to the living room where Irene and the pastor were watching a Seinfeld rerun. The pastor didn't understand why others thought the show was so funny, I listened as Irene tried to explain it to him.

The pastor couldn't laugh about Jerry, George, Kramer, and Elaine, but a lot of what the old lady said hit the mark with him.

Irene was more or less correct. I was kind of in love with Lisbeth Salander. I was also confused about my feelings.

Only a few weeks before the first time Lisbeth and I made love, I had been with a different woman. She was as beautiful as Lisbeth, and sex with her was as good as with Lisbeth. Until Lisbeth's arrival, I thought I was in love with that real-life woman. Her name is Sally. But suddenly, I wasn't so sure.

"There is no point in being in love with a literary character," I replied to Irene. "I can't marry her. I can't even go with her to where she lives."

"Where does she live?"

"Somewhere in Sweden? Somewhere in your library? I don't know. Or maybe she's just *Stuff* like everything else, according to Jean-Baptiste Adamsberg."

Things became more complicated. For three weeks after that evening with Lisbeth, almost every night another beautiful literary female character turned up. I don't remember all of them and didn't write down their names. Looking back at these events, maybe I should have written them down.

There was Jane Bennet from *Pride and Prejudice*. Rebecca arrived, and the next day Rachel, both are characters created by Daphne du Maurier. Emma from Jane Austen's *Emma* turned up. Anna Karenina turned up, and I don't think she needs an introduction. Sula, however, may need an introduction. She stepped out of a novel of the same name, written by Toni Morrison. I found myself almost speechless when Jane from Charlotte Bronte's *Jane Eyre* took me by the hand. Then there was: Scarlett O'Hara, Emma Bovary, Lolita, Justine, and Catherine Bourne.

It was strange. I can't describe it adequately. I still don't understand my behavior. There is, of course, nothing wrong with sex. There is nothing wrong having sex with a person, woman or man, one has met only an hour earlier; there certainly is nothing wrong with having sex with another partner every night. As long as both want it, go for it. I am not critical of my behavior as far as my sexual activities were concerned, but I'm confused – still confused to this day – about my sexual behavior as far as the women I went to bed with were concerned. They were so unbelievably real, and yet, my common sense told me they couldn't be real. Was I dreaming? Did I have wet dreams? Was I masturbating, lost in my sexual fantasies? The answers are: No! No! No! Everything was real and nothing that has happened since gives me any reason to doubt my experiences.

However, when it happened, my mind told me, *this can't be*. Maybe I should have questioned these women. I should have asked them to help me research what was going on. I should have asked them to return with me to the library and show me exactly where and when it was that they experienced themselves for the first time as women made of flesh and skin and sexual desires. Of course, I didn't do anything of that kind; it might have spoiled everything.

Each time when one of these captivating women arrived, Irene would ask her to have a seat and offer sandwiches, fruit or cake and with it beer, wine, lemonade, tea, or coffee. They all made their choices and then the three of us had a relaxing chat, often about political events in the past; there was never boring small talk.

Then the moment arrived... Each time it was the same moment. The beautiful woman said, "I need a handkerchief." I got up and said, "I'll get you one." The beautiful woman got up as well and said, "I'll come with you."

We went into my bedroom and had sex.

Later, we returned to the living room; I opened a bottle of wine, Irene placed an assortment of cheeses on the table, and the three of us continued talking about politics, art, music and world events of the past.

Around midnight, the beautiful women returned to the library and the old lady went to bed. I stayed up and watched TV, usually for another hour or two before I went to my quarters.

The next morning, Irene got up at around eight, I at ten. She often spoiled me with a delicious breakfast, although sometimes she didn't feel like making breakfast. On those mornings we would go to one of the cafes nearby. Other times she was nowhere to be found in the apartment and I made myself something to eat or went to one of the cafes on my own.

Life was great.

15

They say all good things must come to an end, which is probably true. The last beautiful woman to arrive was Catherine Bourne from Hemingway's *The Garden of Eden*. I had read the book years earlier and had a bourgeois kind-of idea about Catherine that turned out to be wrong. We started to explore each other on my sofa and after half an hour moved to the bedroom. She was the only woman who brought me several times in quick successions to what felt like moments of eternal bliss. What a contradiction! But that's how it felt: moments of eternal bliss.

When we decided that enough was enough we had a shower together and underneath the shower we merged once more. It was as if we both knew that this was the last time between us, and we put everything we had into our last moments. When we finally separated, we ended up sitting in the shower basin with the water still running all over us. We squeezed into a corner hugging each other, when suddenly, I felt sad.

"Can you take me to your world?" I asked.

She shook her head, and we stayed under the shower for a few more minutes, just hugging and stroking each other.

16

The next morning when Irene and I had breakfast, she said, "Hemingway was here last night."

"Hemingway!" I exclaimed. "How is that possible? He's not a literary character. He's a human being and he's dead."

"I asked him the same question and he said there were several books about him in my library. One of them, he said, was so boring that he didn't accept the Ernest Hemingway in that book as his true self. The Hemingway in that book is a literary character and thanks to that unfortunate event, which now turned out to be a fortunate event, he was able to show up in my living room."

"I don't believe it."

"That's what I said, but he insisted that it was true and, after all, there he was standing right in front of me."

"Why didn't you get me?"

"I was on my way to get you when Hemingway interfered. He asked me not to disturb you. You were with one of his favorite female literary characters he said. I don't know how he knew this. Unfortunately, he explained, the novel in which that character appears, *The Garden of Eden*, was published 25 years after his death, and the Catherine in the book didn't quite turn out the way he would have portrayed her if he had finished the book. That's the trouble, he pointed out, if you leave unfinished manuscripts behind, all sorts of things can happen after your departure. But there was nothing that could be done now. At least, he added, we could let the two of you have a good time; Catherine deserved it."

"That's what he said?"

"Almost word for word."

"I think he must have mellowed a bit."

"Could well be. He would be well above hundred by now, although he looked half that age."

"That's the thing about these literary characters; they don't seem to age."

"There is definitely something about being a literary character," Irene replied.

"What did he want?" I asked.

"Ah! That's the truly interesting bit. He wants everything that has been published after his death under his name taken off the market."

"Did he tell you how he thinks this could be achieved?"

"He didn't and I told him he was crazy."

"I don't think that went down well."

"He said he was crazy a long time ago, but these days he's perfectly sane."

"He wasn't upset?"

"No! Not a bit. He pointed out that all the books he had written and published during his lifetime were okay, but the books that were edited and published by others after his death were just not how they should have been."

Fair enough, I thought. But why should this be a problem? The world knows which of his books were published after his death. They are still very good books. Even his memoir *A Moveable Feast* is a great book. His last wife, Mary, who had edited the book, sure, she may have deleted reference to his other wives, especially to Hadley, his first wife, but this is a well-known fact. And beyond that, I had heard there was now a new version of the book available, and was supposedly more in accordance with Hemingway's original manuscript.

"He is a complex man," Irene continued. "I think he is full of regrets."

"What makes you say that?"

"He mentioned Hadley and his children, and that he never had enough time for them."

"This wouldn't change if all the books published after his death were taken off the market."

"No, it wouldn't. We talked about it. He was amazingly open about his life and death. He said, and I'm using his own words, 'I shouldn't have killed myself. Killing yourself achieves nothing.' He wasn't emotional about it. He just stated it as a matter of fact."

"How did you two conclude the conversation? Did you agree that you would try to have half of his work removed from the market?"

"No, I didn't. I think he accepted that it can't be done. In the end, we chatted about Ezra Pound, Fitzgerald, Salinger, and Dos Passos. Well, he talked, I listened, and in the process was superbly entertained. We finished a bottle of Jack Daniel's. Let me correct that; I had two glasses and he had the rest. Shortly after midnight, I guided him to the library where I hoped he would find peace between the pages of whichever book he had emerged from. I felt strangely happy, exhausted and went to bed."

"Arguing, chatting and drinking whiskey with Hemingway, heck, why shouldn't you have felt happy! I envy you."

"Are you saying that you would have preferred two hours with the writer instead of four hours with Catherine?"

"Well," I said, "if you put it that way, I guess somehow things have worked out well for both of us."

17

The police were looking for me. I had a little apartment in the Village, which I hadn't entered since a few weeks after I had moved in with the old lady. When I decided to check it out just to make sure everything was okay I met one of my neighbors on the street in front of the building. She told me the police had been looking for me and that a forensics' team had been inside my apartment. When they left, they sealed the entrance door. For me to enter now would mean I had to break the seal. It could even be that the lock on the door had been replaced and my key would no longer work.

I asked if the police had said anything about why they were looking for me.

No, I was told, they only had asked everybody in the building if they knew where I might have gone.

I thanked my neighbor and appreciated that she didn't ask why the police were interested in me.

There was nothing of importance left in my apartment. Everything I needed, including my second hand BMW, I had moved to my new home within a few weeks after Irene and I had met.

I assumed that from the photos and video recordings that were made of the accident the police had managed to identify me. My picture can be found on the back cover of each of my books.

I decided to return to my new home without first checking out my old home.

18

My girlfriend Sally dumped me. I had told her about the literary characters that turned up at the old lady's apartment. She thought I was trying to make myself look important. I invited her for an evening to show her, but unfortunately that evening turned out to be one when nobody turned up. I talked her into coming the next evening again, and again not one character turned up. She asked me to stop the nonsense and we ended up having an argument. The old lady was present and told her that everything I had said was true, and furthermore that I had had sex with about a dozen of the most beautiful female literary characters ever invented. That was the moment when my girlfriend decided that she was in the company of two crazy people and left. Her last words were, "Grow up, you two!"

The old lady asked her, "How much more do you want me to grow up?"

My girlfriend – more accurately, at this moment she was already my ex-girlfriend – didn't reply.

"She probably wasn't the right one for you," Irene said.

"But she was real."

"What's the difference?"

Good question, I thought. What's the difference? Sally had left the apartment through the entrance door, the literary women had disappeared in the library.

"No big difference," I replied.

The next evening, just as the two evenings before, nobody turned up. I commented that it might all have come to an end. Irene didn't think so.

Later that evening she said, "You know your ex-girlfriend has become a liability."

"I know. She is the only person who could tell the police where they could find me."

"Do you think she knows that the police are looking for you?"

"I don't think so," I replied, "but she will know if for some reason she comes across a police or a news report that has my name or picture."

"What are you going to do about it?"

"Nothing. I'll deal with it when it happens."

"You could get rid of her," the old lady suggested.

"You mean – kill her?"

"Well, that's one option. Since you've done all sorts of terrible things to men before, you might want to consider it."

"You are a terrible old woman," I said. "Since when do you know that I've done unpleasant things to bad men? I was thinking of talking to you about it but never came round to doing it."

"Jesus told me."

"You must be kidding."

"No, no. He mentioned it, but he also said, you wouldn't need to worry about it."

"He's right of course. I don't need to worry about it. I only killed bad, really bad rapists."

"He said so."

"Did he condone it?"

"Not exactly, but he seemed cool about it."

"Cool?"

"Yes."

"He's an interesting man, indeed." Then, I had another thought and added, "The problem of course is, the Jesus you spoke to is the literary one and not the real one. The real one may see things differently."

"I don't think so," the old lady replied.

"Why don't you think so?"

"I think there is only one Jesus; he probably likes books and writers, and sometimes he just enjoys pretending to be a literary character himself."

"Do you hear yourself?"

"So what about your ex-girlfriend?" Irene continued, ignoring my last question. "Are you sure you don't want to do anything about her?"

"If I killed her, do you think Jesus would be cool about that too?"

"Probably not – unless, of course, everything in life happens in accordance with God's will."

"You mean, in the event that everything is predetermined?"

"Yes. In a way," Irene replied.

"What do you mean? In a way?"

"Well, it could be that God has predetermined everything billions of years ago. But it could also be that he just makes up His mind as He goes along. In a way, it means the same."

"If that's the case, everything will happen as it is meant to happen. Our talking won't make a difference," I replied.

"True."

"Next time we see Jesus, should he turn up again, we could ask him if everything in our lives is predetermined, if God makes up His mind about things as we travel along, or if we have a free will."

"You think he knows?" Irene asked.

"Asking doesn't cost anything."

"True. But whatever he tells us, can we be certain that it is the truth?"

"We are talking about Jesus," I replied. "But you are right, there are no guarantees in life."

"There is little point in asking then. Let's just forget all about it," the old lady concluded.

I looked at her, wondering if just now she had provided me with a predetermined answer, or with an answer God had given her spontaneously just now, or an answer that was the result of the workings of a free will.

"What you just said," I decided, "were words that you had to say, words that were unavoidable and predetermined since the occurrence of the Big Bang."

"Don't be silly. There has never been such a ridiculous thing called the Big Bang."

"How do you know?" I asked surprised.

"That's just good common sense," my old and wise friend replied.

I concluded that she was right. I just wasn't sure whether or not my conclusion was predetermined.

Irene's next question brought me back to what our discussion was all about. "So what are you going to do about your ex-girlfriend? You don't want to end up in jail."

"I'll do absolutely nothing and I won't end up in jail."

"How can you be so certain?"

"Do you remember what Lisbeth Salander said about God?"

"I do. She said *God is everybody and everything*."

"That's why I know it. Sometimes, human beings know something with absolute certainty without any rational explanation. The explanation is incorporated in this definition: *God is everybody and everything.* That's why I know it."

The next day, two police officers arrived. When Irene let them in, they asked her if a writer by the name of Eberhardt Walker was living with her. As it happened, Pursewarden was also present.

19

At the time when the police arrived at Irene's place, I found myself in the Bronx at a location which shall remain undisclosed. Sitting on a chair in front of me was a man in his forties. His skin was white, his face was clean shaven and he was well-dressed. He didn't deny that he had raped a young woman in her mid-thirties a week earlier.

He wasn't an ugly man, but he wasn't good-looking either. A bit overweight and with a nose that was disproportionately large for his face. He was articulate in an arrogant way and made it quite clear that he didn't feel responsible for what had happened. "I haven't had a girlfriend in years," he said, "and don't want to have anything to do with prostitutes. Fuck them, but not I.

"I have sexual needs just like every man my age. So I forced that woman to have sex with me. What's the big deal! I had watched her for a few weeks and knew that she was married and had two lovers. So I concluded that she might not be too worried about being in bed with me. She might not like it, but so what? Who gives a damn what a slut like her feels!"

He shouldn't have said that. This callous disregard of a woman's feelings is one of the aspects that I really hate about rape.

"I managed to enter her apartment when she was alone, and I told her what I had come for. She screamed at me right away and ran to the kitchen from where she returned with a knife. I took the knife away from her and held my hand over her mouth. She bit me, scratched me, hit me, and kept screaming like she was about to go mad. I hit her on her head with an empty flower vase. She stopped screaming and crashed to the floor. There was blood coming from between her hair. Amazingly, the vase was still okay. She was alive, unconscious, so I undressed her and had sex with her."

"You didn't think," I asked him, "that you had gone too far and that things were heading in the wrong direction and you just should have left?"

"No way!" he replied. "This was a perfect opportunity."

"And what then?"

"She regained consciousness and instead of letting me finish, she started screaming and fighting again. How can you fuck a woman under such circumstances? She was a tough slut, and I had no choice and hit her again with the flower vase. This time the vase broke into pieces. Maybe I hit her a bit too hard."

"You killed her."

"I found out about it the next day."

"When you found out, how did you feel about it?" I asked.

"There was nothing I could do."

"So how did you feel about it?" I asked again.

"I didn't feel much, to tell you the truth."

"You have raped women before, haven't you?"

I could see he didn't like the turn of our conversation. He had been willing to confess to that one rape because he knew I had all the evidence and denying it wouldn't have assisted his case.

He was in my hands, sitting on a kitchen chair in front of me in his own kitchen, with each of his hands handcuffed to the arms of the chair.

"How many women have you raped?"

"Not many."

"Is this the first one you killed?"

He wouldn't look at me and didn't reply. I asked him again. He mumbled something about he didn't know and did it really matter. I had heard enough and my decision was made.

"Look," I said, "you could be right. You may not be responsible for what you did. Maybe God or the devil or your upbringing or the environment or our time or the way the world has become is responsible. We don't know. I just want to make sure that you don't rape a woman again. I have a tablet here and if you take it, your sexual desire will be greatly reduced and of a nature that you can control without having to rape someone.

He looked at me suspiciously as they all had done before him. There was no hurry. We talked about if for a few minutes until I had convinced him that the tablet was truly harmless; that taking the tablet was definitely better than handing him over to the police. That last suggestion that I could hand him over to the police did the trick. It always did.

I gave him a few Mexican Euthanasia drugs, removed the handcuffs and led him to his bed where he died peacefully soon afterwards.

20

When I returned to Irene's apartment it was shortly after ten pm. Irene was not at home, and I went straight to the library, made myself comfortable in one of the library chairs, and started to speak.

"Look there are a few things that have to come to an end. I will list them for your benefit and to avoid misunderstandings." At this point I stopped, got up, and walked to one of the book shelves. I took out a big book entitled *The Bible* and placed it on the table in front of the chair to which I returned.

"Just so that everybody has a clear understanding," I continued, "about to whom my speech is addressed. You all, of course, are welcome to listen. Also feel free to comment. Feel free to support me, or to disagree with me.

"I had to deal with another rapist today and ensured that he won't rape anybody again. I've stopped counting how many times I've had to do the same before. Yes, you understood correctly. I said *I had to do it*. I had no choice. I don't feel responsible for what I did. It was the same with the man I had to kill today. He, too, told me that he didn't feel responsible for what he did. He was probably right, but I killed him anyway. It's not that I see myself as someone who thinks he has to bring justice to this world. I simply *had to do* something to make sure that this man can't rape and kill more women. I could have cut his penis off of course, but I think that would have been much crueler than to put him asleep. Besides, even without a penis, he could still do bad things to women. You may know that I have reduced the size of some penises before, but I never felt quite right about it.

"I said at the beginning, there are a few things that have to come to an end. Men raping women has to end. Just look at what's going on in places like India, Egypt, in other African countries and here in New York City, my home town. What some men do to women is barbaric. Quite frankly, I don't understand how *you* can allow that to happen. What is it? One vicious rape a second? Or is one vicious rape every ten seconds? For heaven's sake! Just one rape a day would be 365 rapes a year too many. *This has got to stop!*

"Men raping women has to stop. That I have to kill rapists has to stop. But how can it stop? I can't just quit doing what I have to do as long as I receive phone calls telling me about what's going on in my former neighborhood. The very moment men stop raping women, there is no longer a need for me to kill men. It is as simple as that.

"But there's more. Just look at what else is happening all over the globe! There is terrorism, violence, extremism, radicalism, racism, war, bombings, kidnappings, assassinations, torture, suffering, agony, murder, massacres, killings in the name of religion, priests molesting children, hundreds of thousands of different kinds of crime, hunger, deprivation, starvation, famine, emotional cruelty, anguish, misery and indifference wherever one looks. Switch on the TV and there it is. Surf the Internet and you find these heart wrenching stories by the millions. Open the newspaper and show me one page without something about crime and misery."

"This has got to stop!"

"Now!"

"For once and for ever!"

21

Pursewarden said to the police officers, "I'm Eberhardt Walker, the writer."

For a second or two there was silence. Then, before the police officers could say anything, the old lady pushed Pursewarden aside and said, "No! He's not. His name is Pursewarden."

Pursewarden looked surprised. He wasn't an easily flustered man. By pretending that he was me, he clearly thought that he did the old lady and me a favor. However, Irene's mind worked at the speed of light and after she had assessed the various possible scenarios and consequences that might result from Pursewarden's claim that he was me, she decided that a slightly different approach might turn out more favorable in the long term.

The police officers didn't look surprised. It's quite possible that they were used to people claiming they were someone they weren't. Or the other way round, that they weren't who they claimed they were. "Well," one of the officers said, looking at the man who usually lives between the covers of a book in the old lady's library, "it would make things a lot easier if you two could agree about whether you are Mr. Walker or Mr. Pursewarden, and once you have agreed, I would like to see identification."

"I'm Eberhardt Walker, the writer," Pursewarden insisted. He added, "Walker, like Johnny Walker, my preferred whisky."

"Not like Jack Daniels?" the police officer asked. He seemed to have a sense of humor.

"He's Pursewarden, the writer," Irene pointed out.

"Two writers, I see," replied the police officer. He then arrived at an amazingly logical possible explanation. Addressing Pursewarden he said,

"I suspect Eberhardt Walker is your real name and Pursewarden is your literary name; the name under which you publish your books. Right? And by the way, is Pursewarden your first name or your surname?"

"Wrong!" replied the old lady. "Pursewarden is his literary name, that's correct and that's the only name under which he's known; he was invented by Lawrence Durrell and has nothing to do with Eberhardt Walker."

"Right!" replied Pursewarden who seemed to enjoy the game. "I am Eberhardt and Pursewarden is my literary name."

"Wrong!" repeated the old lady. "He's an imposter. In fact, he committed suicide a few decades ago. He doesn't even exist."

Now the second police officer, a young female, decided that she should add something to the conversation. "He can't have committed suicide," she said, looking at Irene. "He is here, alive and well. Maybe he attempted to commit suicide. Is that what you meant, madam?"

"Yes, that's what she meant," said Pursewarden. "Don't take her seriously. Her memory is no longer what it used to be; she's getting on a bit."

"I'm inclined to take you both to the police station," the older male officer contemplated, but he was quickly interrupted by Pursewarden, "Oh no, sir, that's a bad idea. She needs to take her medication every hour, and she's also expecting a visit by her medical practitioner. If something happens to her at the police station, believe me, you wouldn't like to be responsible."

"What should happen to her?"

"She suffers from epileptic episodes."

"He's a liar, liar, liar... Don't believe a word he says!"

The policeman made his decision. Looking at Pursewarden, he said, "You come with us, the lady stays here."

"Wise decision," Pursewarden commented and smiled.

"Not sure why you should be so happy about this," the policeman said and handcuffed the literary character.

The two police officers took Pursewarden away. After they had left, the old lady called her lawyer. He was still in his office and said he would be happy to see her. She called a taxi and left her apartment ten minutes later.

22

After I had said everything I had to say, I stayed in the library for another twenty minutes, before I returned to the living room. Pursewarden was watching TV, a repeat of an old Frasier show. I asked him if he wanted something to drink. Instead of answering my question he said, "I think I'm in love with Daphne."

"She's quite a successful lady," I replied. "English, just like you."

"I'm not interested in her real life. Daphne is a fictional character, just like me. It's on that level that I love her."

There's no other level for you, I thought. I felt a bit sorry for him. Then I thought I could be wrong. He looked tired and less assured than how I remembered him from his previous visits.

"We've met."

"What do you mean?" I asked.

"Daphne and I've met. We were lovers, albeit for one night only."

"How is that possible?" At the moment I asked this question, I thought of the one-night affairs I had with a dozen fictional characters. Still, I was wondering, Daphne Moon was both a fictional character and a real life actress by the name of Jane Leeves. How could these two characters be kept apart? I mean, if Pursewarden spent a night with Daphne, what would Jane's reaction have been?

"Fictional characters meet all over the world, didn't you know that?"

"I didn't. Could you elaborate please?"

"It's just another universe," Pursewarden explained. "A few years ago, I spent a week in Tokyo with Nakata."

"Nakata? Isn't he one of Haruki Murakami's characters from *Kafka on the Shore*?"

"Yes, he is. He's a very interesting, wise, philosophical man."

"He had lost his memory and had something to do with lost cats, if I remember correctly?"

"It's all a bit metaphysical."

"Who else have you met? I mean what other literary characters have you met in this – how shall I put it? – other universe?"

"Call it the literary universe. I don't know how many other literary characters I've met there. Thousands. It would be like asking you how many human beings have you met since you were born."

"Okay… But tell me, there are fictional literary characters that were created decades ago, like you, there are the ones that are being created right now as we speak and there are the ones that were created centuries ago. And, not to forget, there are fictional characters from TV shows, movies, Internet blogs, and who knows what other sources." I had to catch my breath.

"Yes?"

"Do they all live together and mix happily in this…, *literary universe*?"

"Yes, pretty much."

"Wow! That sounds exciting," I couldn't help saying. Then, upon a bit of reflection, "Why do you bother visiting this world? My world? I mean, I know, most of you want to have parts of the novels from which you originated rewritten. But why? What's the point of it? It seems you have all the excitement, entertainment and adventurers you could ask for already. You are famous in this world and you can meet – and even have sex with – the most interesting and beautiful characters ever invented. What's the problem?"

"The problem is free will."

"Free will?" I asked perplexed.

At this moment, we could hear the entrance door to the apartment and a few seconds later the old lady walked into the living room. She looked briefly at Pursewarden and said, "I didn't expect you back so soon." Then, looking at me, she continued, "How about an Ancient Cognac?"

I knew what she was talking about and went to my quarters where I had a bottle of an ancient drink with a value that can't be expressed in monetary terms. It's a bottle that's several hundred years old, that had rested for most of these years on the bottom of the ocean and that had probably nothing to do with cognac. The old lady and I call it Ancient Cognac for conveniences' sake.

I had stolen it from a very, very rich man a few weeks earlier. He was unwise enough, or maybe ill-advised, to have it displayed at an exhibition of seldom and rare alcoholic beverages. It was, without a doubt, the center piece of the exhibition. Very little was known about the bottle, except that it was hundreds of years old and contained, most likely, a liquor or fortified wine of some sort. It could have been vinegar or poison by now. As long as the bottle remained sealed, there was no way of knowing what it was exactly. The very rich man never bothered to open it and taste it. I guess he looked at it as an investment or, more likely, as something to show off with.

The old lady and I had walked through the exhibition and when we stood in front of the bottle – which, as you would expect, was located behind bullet proof glass and surrounded by cameras and security equipment – the old lady said to me, "I would love to know what it tastes like. Is it for sale?"

I had read the catalogue and told her what was known about the bottle and that it wasn't for sale.

"Well, I guess," she said, "in that case, you'll just have to steal it."

Was she joking or serious? I had no idea.

"No problem," I replied and we left it at that and returned home half an hour later.

A few days later, we watched CNN and there was a report about that particular bottle of alcohol. The night before the last day of the exhibition someone had found their way into the exhibition hall and had, with the help of a good deal of explosives, stolen the bottle. It happened extraordinarily fast the reporter pointed out. By the time security arrived, there was quite a bit of damage and no bottle.

"What a pity," the old lady said, "now you can't steal it anymore. Someone beat you to it."

"Not unless a burglar has been in my quarters," I replied and got up and returned a minute later with the bottle.

"Well done!" she said. I could see she was pretty surprised, perhaps even impressed.

"What do you think?" I asked. "Shall we open it?"

"What else is there to be done?"

I opened the bottle and held it to my nose. I breathed in, slowly absorbing the myriad of ancient messages I could detect. I fetched two cognac glasses and poured a few drops of the golden fluid into one glass. I breathed in once more. I took the glass to my mouth and let the fluid linger on my tongue, allowing the flavor to take hold of every cell in my body. I closed my eyes and stood in silence. I don't know for how long. I opened my eyes and vaguely realized that the world had changed. But I did not want to define that change. I poured the golden fluid into each of the two cognac glasses until each glass was filled approximately one inch from the bottom. I handed one glass to my friend, the old lady.

We looked at each other. We didn't speak. We lifted the glasses. We allowed them to just slightly thump together. For the next hour, we were sitting beside each other, our eyes closed, every now and then sipping from the century old golden fluid in the glasses in our hands.

When we opened our eyes, the old lady said, "Please take the bottle to your quarters. Use it wisely."

I got up and took the bottle to my quarters and placed it on one of my book shelves between two books: *You Get So Alone at Times That It Just Makes Sense* by Charles Bukowski and *On the Road: The Original Scroll* by Jack Kerouac. I hope Charles and Jack forgive me for the temptation I may have caused.

I was just about to get up and fetch the bottle of Ancient Cognac from my quarters when Irene changed her mind. "On second thought," she said, "give me a glass of George Dickel please. It would not be wise to drink the most delicious and expensive stuff in the world just because my lawyer has lost his marbles."

"Anything serious?" I enquired.

I poured her a substantial George Dickel Tennessee.

"I don't know yet, but first let's talk about this gentleman here." She pointed at Pursewarden and continued, "I didn't expect to find you here. Shouldn't you be in jail?"

"No," Pursewarden replied, "I had a friendly conversation with the two police officers and soon afterwards they gave me a lift home."

"Wow!" I exclaimed. "What have you done?" I also wanted to ask him about his home. Where was his home? But I decided that can wait.

"He pretended to be you," Irene said.

"Did he? How interesting!"

"He meant well," Irene added, this time with a smile.

They told me what had happened whilst I had arranged for the transfer of a rapist from this world to the next. They went through the details about their discussion with the two police officers. They made an effort to repeat word by word their argument in front of the police officers about Pursewarden's identity. I couldn't help but laugh out loud when they arrived at the point when Pursewarden convinced the officers that the old lady needed to take medication every hour, and to take her to the police station could be more trouble than what it was worth.

"So far so good," Irene concluded, "but now let's talk about how things continued. The last time I saw you" – she pointed at the literary character – "you were being taken away in handcuffs."

"Yes, that was a new experience to me. But tell me, why didn't you go along with my game and allow me to be Eberhardt?" As he said this he looked at me. "Why did you insist that I was Pursewarden, a literary character from a book that was written decades ago? Nobody would ever believe that."

"That was the idea. I didn't want to be believed. I wanted to appear like an old woman who had a few loose screws in her head."

"I'd say you succeeded brilliantly," Pursewarden replied. He looked amused.

"Of course I succeeded. And you helped me. When you told the police officers that I suffered from epileptic fits, there was no doubt left in their minds that I was a crazy old woman."

"Okay, but why?"

"Well, I was wondering how this would all work out in the long run. You pretended to be Eberhardt Walker. I insisted that you were a fictional character. Obviously, I expected that they wouldn't believe me and that you'd be led away in handcuffs. But I asked myself, 'what will happen when the police realize that you weren't who they thought you were?' If I had agreed that you were Eberhardt, they could have returned and accused me of collusion. However, by telling them the truth, I could not be accused of anything."

"Except of being crazy," I threw in with a chuckle. I understood Irene's thought processes.

"Exactly," she continued. "I said to myself, however this game may continue for the two of you, I would have to remain free. This was important. Firstly, I'm a bit too old for prison. But secondly and more importantly, whatever might happen from here on, I can be more useful as a free woman than as an imprisoned woman."

"Brilliant!" I acknowledged. "So, the police thought you, Pursewarden, were me and they took you away, and as it seems, you returned within a couple of hours. How did you manage that?"

"Yeah, within about three hours I was back home watching Frasier. I may add, I wanted to return to my real home, the library, but just when I was about to open the door, I heard you giving your speech."

"I had a few things to get off my chest about the state of the world, and I hope that Jesus or God or both of them paid attention."

"I thought it would be something like that. Do you think they listened?"

"Probably not," I answered.

"Don't change the topic," the old lady interfered. "I want to know what happened at the police station."

"We didn't go to a police station."

This is getting really interesting.

Pursewarden continued. "Once in the police car, I suggested that we have dinner at the Le Bernardin."

"That's one of the most expensive restaurants in town," I commented.

"Yes, I believe it is. I invited them, and they didn't need a lot of persuading. We had great meals. Absolutely superb. And the wine was just perfect."

"That must have cost you a grand or more. Where did you get the money from to pay for such a feast?"

"Oh, I have lots of money," Pursewarden replied casually. "Money is not *the issue* in my life."

I felt like asking him what *the issue* was, when I remembered. He wanted that part of Durrell's work rewritten that was about his suicide. I wondered why. He was alive and well, what did it matter what Lawrence Durrell had written decades ago? But I kept quiet. I didn't want to mix reality and fiction, although I had the feeling that that was already happening.

Pursewarden continued. "We enjoyed our dinner and our company. As we ate, we talked about the world today, about the economy, inflation, and the inadequacy of police salaries. I realized life was not easy for these two people. And so, since I have a lot more money than I need, I suggested to them that I could give each one of them half a million dollars and in return they could delete my little infringement from their database."

"You mean my infringement?" I interrupted.

"Yes, of course. I was you."

"How could you produce a million dollars just like that? You didn't have it in your wallet, did you?"

"Very funny. We went to an Internet café where I set up two accounts at a Panamanian bank for them. I'm a customer of that bank and have a special code that allows me to do that. I then transferred half a million dollars into each of their accounts from one of my Swiss bank accounts. The whole procedure took twenty minutes. I explained to them how they could access their money without creating suspicion. What else? They gave me a lift home and everybody was happy."

"Thank you!" I said and shook his hand. "If everybody's happy, then I'm happy."

"That's it?" the old lady asked.

"Yeah. I guess so," I replied. "You got me into this slightly tricky situation, which I'm very grateful for, and Pursewarden got me out of it, which I'm equally grateful for."

"Is it really that simple?"

"I think so. Stealing that car and everything that followed brought excitement into my life. Pursewarden's generous donation to two police officers returned a certain degree of peace of mind to my life. I'm a happy man."

I got up and asked if anybody else would like a beer or something else to drink. Pursewarden opted for a beer and Irene for a glass of water. I served them both before I pointed out that there were still two issues I thought we should talk about.

23

"What issues?" they asked simultaneously.

"What happened at your lawyer's office?" I asked looking at Irene. You arrived home and asked for alcohol before you said hi. That's not like you."

Looking at Pursewarden, I asked, "How on earth does a literary character from around the 1930s obtain a Swiss bank account? How does he know how to set up online bank accounts in Panama? And what I really want to know is how did you get a million dollars into your Swiss bank account in the first place?"

"Several million," Pursewarden corrected me.

"Several million! How many million exactly?"

"About seventeen, unless one of my duplicates has deposited or withdrawn something within the last few hours."

"One of your duplicates?"

"This is interesting," the old lady interrupted. "Let's talk about Pursewarden's duplicates and bank accounts first, then I'll tell all about my lawyer."

"That's quickly explained," Pursewarden replied. "I'm not the only Pursewarden in your world. Wherever you find one of Lawrence Durrell's books in which I appear, you could theoretically have my literary character leaving the book and mixing with people like yourself."

"What a nightmare!" I couldn't help but shout. "This means there could be hundreds of thousands of Pursewardens running around."

"Theoretically, yes. But the real figure is much smaller."

"Tens of thousands?" I asked.

"At any given time about half a dozen or less," the fictional writer replied.

"Why not more?" Irene enquired.

"We don't want to make things confusing for ourselves."

"I don't believe this," I said and got up to get myself another George Dickel. "They don't want to make things confusing for themselves.

Pursewarden, do you hear yourself? Just having you here – one Pursewarden! – is bloody confusing."

"From your perspective, yes, I can see that; but not from the perspective of the four Pursewardens that are outside their books at this very moment."

"Are you four in contact with each other? Or how do you know that right now there are another three of you walking around somewhere on this planet?"

"You could say we are in contact, although to me it doesn't feel as if there is more than one of us. At this moment, two Pursewardens are outside their books in Germany, one in the UK, and myself here with you in New York. I know that there are four of us, but we feel as if we were just one man. For example, if I make a little effort and listen to what's going on inside myself, then I know what each of my duplicates in Germany and the UK is doing, thinking, and feeling. Equally, they can put themselves into a position in which they know what I'm doing, thinking, and feeling. We function in complete harmony."

"In *complete* harmony! Are you sure?"

"Well… sometimes we disagree. I guess a bit like every human being, from what I have heard; one part inside you wants one thing and another part something else. What do you call it? Emotional conflicts within? One part wants to buy shares, another part says that's too risky, one part wants to eat a cake, another part says that's unhealthy."

"One part inside me is calling this conversation a nightmare, another part tells me that this conversation can't be. Which part is right?" I wondered.

"What about a break?"

"Good idea."

"What about watching Frasier?"

"You mean, you want to watch Daphne," I replied.

24

We didn't talk about the old lady's experience with her lawyer until the next day. We watched Frasier, Niles, Martin, Eddie, Roz, and of course Daphne until around midnight. Even Irene stayed up.

"I guess the lawyer stuff can wait till tomorrow," she said when we left the big living room and headed towards our bedrooms.

"I think I'll have a quick shower," I said, more to myself than anybody else. Then a thought occurred to me and I asked Pursewarden, "What about you and the other literary characters?"

"What do you mean?" he asked.

"I'm just wondering… and I hope I'm not too inquisitive… What are you doing once you have closed the library door behind you? I guess you return to your book, although I can't imagine how. But what then? Do you have a place to go to? A home? A shower? A bed?"

Pursewarden stopped, and for the first time, I noticed that he had a very serious side to his personality. He seemed to look inside himself and at me simultaneously. We were standing a few feet from the library door.

"Do I have a place to go to? A home? A shower? A bed?" Pursewarden repeated.

I said nothing. Maybe I shouldn't have asked. Not now, anyway.

"Yes," the fictitious man replied. "Yes."

He turned and disappeared in the library. For a moment, I felt like following him but I heard a voice say, "If you do that, you'll never see him again."

I looked around, but couldn't see anybody. A few minutes later, I had returned to my room to take a shower. I spent another two hours writing on a novel I had started a few weeks earlier. I rewarded myself with a sip from my very special Ancient Cognac. It was three am when I went to bed. As it is usually the case with me, I fell asleep within minutes and woke up, at peace with myself and the world, seven hours later.

Irene and I met for lunch at noon in the kitchen. We enjoyed eating and talking about things in the large and comfortably furnished kitchen. I hadn't had breakfast because I had worked on my novel for a few hours after I'd woken up. Irene had a housekeeper, a woman in her mid-forties. Her name was Sue, and she was happy to assist with whatever tasks had to be done. She was a brilliant cook and whatever food she prepared – be it just sandwiches, a sophisticated five course dinner, or a delicious cake

– I always felt like saying that it was the best I've ever eaten in my life. Often I said it. Sue felt that I meant it, and it made both of us happy.

We were half way through lunch, a sweet German dish called *Ofenschlupfer*, when Irene said, "I met Mickey Haller at my lawyer's office. Do you know him?"

Mickey Haller sounds familiar," I replied, "but I can't remember where I've heard that name."

"Have you ever read Michael Connelly?"

"Oh no! I don't believe this!" was all I could say for a moment. Mickey Haller is a character from one of Connelly's novels. "He is referred to as the Lincoln Lawyer."

"Yes, the Lincoln Lawyer," the old lady confirmed.

"And you met him in your lawyer's office?"

"I did. And I was really pissed off about it."

"That's not like you. What happened?"

"Terrence Toplaw has been my lawyer for the past forty years," Irene explained. "We have made millions together. He's an expert in business amalgamation laws, which is where we made our money. I can tell you more about it some other time. But what I really appreciated about him most, apart from his legal acumen, is his ability to analyze everything I've ever discussed with him. He can identify in minutes without fail, the aspects of a topic that matter most. You can talk to him about insider share trading, an unusual cake recipe, or the melting of the polar ice caps, and he will point out to you whatever the crux of the topic is. He is in his late sixties and one of the most intelligent men I've ever met. He is overweight, looks unhealthy and is not very talkative, which is unusual for a lawyer. But that's how he is.

"I went to him shortly after Pursewarden, pretending that he was you, was taken away by the police. I wanted to run what had happened past someone neutral, someone intelligent and with a good grip on reality."

"And you met the Lincoln Lawyer?" I interrupted her.

"Not right away. I started with Terrence Toplaw, telling him about the literary characters that had turned up here in recent months. I expected him to interrupt me and tell me to seek the assistance of a psychiatrist. But he just listened, he didn't even ask questions, which was very unusual.

"I moved on to the events of the evening and told him about the arrival of the two police officers, about the deadly accident on the crossing where you and I met and about the theft of the dead idiot's car. I told him about Pursewarden's insistence that he was you and that the police officers had taken him away."

"What did he say?"

"Nothing. He didn't say a word for quite a while, until I waved several times my hand in front of his face to find out if he was sleeping or awake. He was awake, or maybe I woke him up, I'm not so sure. Anyhow, he finally said 'I can't help you.'"

"I can't help you?"

"Yeah, that's what he said."

"What then?"

"I asked him if he had lost his marbles."

"Oh, oh."

"He replied, and he was now returning to his old self, that he hadn't lost his marbles, just as he knew that I hadn't lost my marbles. But that this was a case outside his expertise. He said, word by word, 'I'm not doing literary characters.' I asked him if he couldn't at least express an opinion, however speculative it might be. I needed to know, I told him, how to get Pursewarden out of jail without being locked up as a lunatic. No, he insisted, he couldn't. There was nothing in the law books that dealt with literary characters who pretended to be humans and there was no advice, not even a suggestion that he could offer."

"Do you think he thought you were a lunatic?"

"That thought flashed through my mind," the old lady admitted, "but I dismissed it because a few moments earlier he'd stated quite clearly that he knew that I hadn't lost my marbles. Reflecting on this statement, I asked him now how he could be so sure that the problem wasn't just in my head – a figment of my imagination."

Here Irene paused for a while until I prompted her by saying, "You still with me?"

"Sure," she said with a smile, "I'm here, fully awake."

"And?"

"He looked at me and said that he was no longer a man who could confidently separate figments of imaginations from reality, especially when literary characters were concerned. So I shouldn't worry about that aspect. At this point, I felt a mixture of anger and concern and asked him to be honest to me and come to the point.

"The point was, he said, that he had a literary character matter to deal with on his own and had no idea how to go about it."

"Ha!" I laughed, "The Lincoln Lawyer had appeared to him. Right?"

"Spot on. About every second day, he told me, Mickey Haller, better known as the Lincoln Lawyer, visited him and asked him for legal advice."

"About what?"

"Cases he was working on in his fictional world."

"Shouldn't he go to Michael Connolly with these cases? After all, Connolly is his creator and accordingly, one should think, has to provide ongoing support."

"My lawyer replied that was exactly what he had told him. But the Lincoln Lawyer didn't want to hear it. His relationship with the author was tense, he said. He didn't want to go into details."

"We live in a crazy world," was all I could think of to say.

"You can say that twice," Irene agreed, before she continued, "Anyhow, I couldn't get any word of advice from my lawyer, and we ended up in a bit of an argument when I asked him what was the point of me paying him an annual retainer of hundred thousand dollars if he couldn't think of even one sentence of advice."

"What did he reply?"

"He was upset and said that he regretted that I was unhappy with the level of service that he could offer; but if I was interested, he could refer me to another lawyer who might have experience in dealing with legal matters concerning literary characters."

"The Lincoln Lawyer! Did he seriously suggest that you should see the Lincoln Lawyer?"

"That's exactly what he did."

"And then?"

"I told him that I was pissed off. These were the exact words I used. But then, just when I got up to leave, a man entered the office and introduced himself as Mickey Haller, the Lincoln Lawyer."

"You can't be serious."

"I am."

"What happened then?"

"I decided that either the world, or I, had gone crazy. So I left."

PART 3:

The twenty five literary characters and time travelling

25

Things were reasonably quiet for a couple of weeks. I couldn't find any Michael Connolly books in Irene's library and bought a few, including *The Lincoln Lawyer*. I thought it wouldn't hurt to get to know him, but he didn't turn up. Maybe he only wanted to mix with lawyers and wasn't interested in ordinary people like me. That was okay.

Then, there was that evening when twenty five literary characters walked into the living room. The first one to arrive was Jay Gatsby. "Don't be alarmed," he said. "You'll have a few visitors this evening, a few of my fictional friends. We would like to discuss something with you." The way he addressed the old lady and me made it clear that he meant both of us. "I hope this is okay," he continued, "but if this evening is not convenient, we can arrange another evening."

"This evening is fine," Irene replied. It was only half past seven and Irene asked if he and his friends would stay for dinner.

"No, no!" Gatsby emphasized, "We don't want you to go to that much trouble. Cooking for twenty five people would be quite a bit of work. I couldn't…"

"Don't be ridiculous," the old lady interrupted him. "I'm not going to cook for you lot. I'm going to order Pizza and let you pay for it. I'm happy to furnish the wine or beer, whatever you and your friends prefer. Both go well with Pizza."

"I'm afraid I don't have a cent on me," Gatsby replied. He looked slightly embarrassed.

"I'm sure your mate Pursewarden is happy to lend you a few dollars for a few days."

Gatsby looked increasingly uncomfortable and replied, "I'm afraid he won't. I owe him a lot of money, and he knows that he will never get it back. He won't lend me more."

"Why won't he get it back?" I asked. "I thought you're a wealthy man."

"I decided decades ago that I don't want to have anything to do with money anymore. Throughout my existence, money has never brought me happiness. In the literary world in which I now live, money is not a necessity."

"Don't you need money to buy food, to buy a house or pay rent, to buy gas for your car, and for thousands of other things?"

"No. Some of us in our fictional existence use money just the way you do, either habitually or for the fun of it, but for the majority of us money doesn't really exist."

"Wow!" I said. "What a life! No money worries. Unfortunately, this system doesn't work here in New York. I'll pay for the Pizza."

"Very kind of you," Jay replied.

Half an hour later, we had twenty five literary characters in the room. There was Füssun from Orhan Pamuk's *Museum of Innocence*. Füssun wasn't happy with Kemal's obsessive love. Everybody who's read the book will probably agree with her. Füssun insisted that the ending of the novel would have to be rewritten.

Santiago, you know about him, wanted to return from his fishing trip with the marlin intact and not with the skeleton of the fish. I told him Hemingway won't be happy with such a major rewrite of his most famous book. "The fictional Hemingway is working on the rewrite as we speak," Santiago replied with a big smile. "How come?" I asked surprised. "He thinks there will be a hell of a hullabaloo once two radically different versions of the book are on the market. That's something he wants to watch." It seemed the famous author had more humor than I would have given him credit for. "But he wants to be sure that the rewrite is a real Hemingway rewrite. He is sick of other people rewriting his books," Santiago added. Fair enough, I thought.

There were the literary characters I had mentioned earlier: Pursewarden, Jay Gatsby, Henry Miller's second wife, June, whom he called Mona in his books, Jean-Baptiste Adamsberg, Lisbeth Salander, Josef Bloch, Alexei Ivanovich, Philip Carey, that criminal from an Edgar Wallace novel, Walter Faber and his daughter Sabeth, Iris from Margaret Atwood's *The Blind Assassin*, Lady Brett Ashley from Hemingway's novel *Fiesta*, that poor character who had his penis bitten off by Garp's wife, and of course, not to forget, there was Jesus.

Jesus only stayed for five minutes, though. Before he left, he told everyone that after thorough consideration, he had decided to commission

Christian and Christina, two literary ghost-writers, to rewrite *The Bible*. This could take five years or longer, he pointed out, as the Bible is quite extensive. Everybody nodded. Once he was happy with the revised version of the book, he said, he'd be back and we could discuss what to do next.

Lolita from Vladimir Nabokov's book by the same title thought that the book was okay at the time when it was first published in 1955, but it no longer satisfied. "Why not?" asked the old lady. "Because it is politically incorrect," said Lolita. "The only thing that's politically incorrect is your age," argued Irene. Lolita considered for a moment what the old lady had said before she replied, "That's an interesting thought; maybe all I need to do is change my age from twelve to sixteen."

Florentino Ariza and Fermina Daza from Gabriel García Márquez's *Love in the Time of Cholera* had only one wish, which sounded simple enough on the surface, but which I knew would result in an entirely different book: they wanted to be married, but not only that, they wanted to be married before the age of forty.

The doctor's wife in *Blindness* by José Saramago insisted adamantly that she and her husband were not meant to appear in the book at all. José had made a mistake. At the time when people in the city went blind, she and her husband were meant to be in Sweden. "I'm going to replace my husband and me," she said, "with another couple." I commented, "I guess that other couple won't like to be in the book either, whoever they are." She replied, "I will replace them with an old couple that is already blind before everybody else goes blind, and I'll let them die as early as possible. That's the only humane thing to do." I didn't mention all the other blind people. I thought this would make things too complicated.

In *The Tin Drum* by Günter Grass, the protagonist is Oskar Matzerath, a dwarf. All in all, he said he was happy with the book, only he would have preferred to have had sex with a few more women, especially younger ones. "That should be possible; what do you think?" he asked me. "Without messing up the book." I couldn't see why not.

Pearl S. Buck's *The Good Earth* is one of those books I would not be brave enough to change one comma. Wang Lung, the book's major character, said he would like to change the way he looked at life during the early and final parts of the book. I was wondering if I should feel worried.

Saleem Sinai, the protagonist from Salman Rushdie's *Midnight's Children*, felt that too much political trauma had been loaded onto his shoulders. He wanted to be endowed with a different attitude. "I wished," he said to the old lady, "there was a bit of Buddhism in my blood." When she asked him to be a bit more specific, he said that at times he wanted to be more detached from all the political nonsense that was going on around him.

The one hundred year old Allan Karlsson from Jonas Jonasson's novel *The 100-Year-Old Man Who Climbed Out the Window and Disappeared* was a bit of an exception. He said, "There are a few translation inconsistencies in one of the foreign editions of the book; they need to be fixed." He didn't tell us which foreign edition he was referring to.

Carlos Ruiz Zafón's Daniel Sempere was also there. I forgot what he wasn't happy with.

The group of literary characters selected Jay Gatsby as their spokesperson. Like the gentleman he was, he asked the old lady if this was okay with her. She told him it was okay with her for the time being, but she reserved the right to change her mind should he be wanting.

"Really?" he asked. "You think I might be wanting?"

"One never knows and your reputation is not exactly very transparent, in my opinion," Irene replied.

Gatsby looked embarrassed. Irene told him not to be so damn sensitive. She would have said exactly the same, no matter who'd be the group's spokesperson. "Mr. Gatsby," she advised him, "it's always good to leave a backdoor open."

Gatsby looked over at me. I could see he was worried that I might throw another spanner into the works, albeit, it has to be said, Irene's spanner was nothing else but an expression of her sense of humor, which obviously was lost on Jay. I just nodded and said, "It's all yours Jay."

"All these people," Gatsby started, "they have..."

People? I thought, it seems we have to redefine the definition of people. You lot are not exactly people according to the existing dictionary definition; you are imaginations that have somehow managed to intrude into the world of people.

"...one thing in common, they want the stories of their creations changed."

"Forget it!" the old lady threw in. "Time travelling hasn't been invented yet. You can't go back and change the past."

"He does it all the time." Daniel Sempere said and pointed at me.

"Do I?"

"Of course! You are a writer. Every time you sit in front of your computer and write a plot, you create fictional reality. The next day, a few days, or sometimes years later you edit your plot, meaning you travel back in time and change the past. Each time you change the past, you also change the present. You do it all the time. In your thrillers, you arrange for someone to be killed, ten thousand words later you change your mind, you do a bit of editing and you bring the dead person back to life. If he is lucky, he stays alive, if he is unlucky you have him killed again."

"That sounds terrible. I've never looked at it that way."

"That's how it is. People like you, Paul Auster, Haruki Murakami, Salman Rushdie, Michael Connelly, Donna Leon, Fred Vargas and Philip Roth and so on, wield immense power and behave like gods without much thinking about the long term consequences your decisions have on the lives of the characters you create. Just look at poor Pursewarden, he committed suicide because Lawrence Durrell liked the idea, but Pursewarden, as we all know, is very unhappy with this part of the book and wants it to be changed."

"Poor Pursewarden!" I exclaimed, not believing what I had heard. "For a start, he is not poor, he is a very wealthy man who can afford to give a million dollars away like other people give ten dollars away, which, I may add, I'm very grateful for. Secondly, Lawrence Durrell may have mentioned somewhere in one of his books that poor Pursewarden killed himself, but we all know what that is, don't we?"

"What is it?"

"It's fiction, for heaven's sake! It didn't really happen. The fact that poor Pursewarden is here, sitting amongst us, alive and enjoying a beer, is proof."

"You don't get it," Daniel Sempere said and looked at me as if I was mentally handicapped.

"What is it I don't get?" I asked.

"It's all about coming to terms with one's past. Just think about it. Half of New York is seeing a psychologist every week because there is something in their past that makes the present difficult and often unbearable. It's the same with Pursewarden and every literary character in this room."

"Just do what the people in New York do," I replied. "Go and see a psychologist. There are lots of novels with good fictional psychologists. Consult them."

At this point, Pursewarden stood up and interjected, "This is quite a logical suggestion, however, there is one problem."

"A big problem," Jay Gatsby confirmed.

"An insurmountable problem," Oskar Matzerath added as further confirmation.

"Stop interrupting and wasting time," the old lady interfered. "What's the bloody big, insurmountable problem with the psychologists?"

"They are no good. They can't help," Pursewarden answered.

"How do you know that? Have you seen any?"

"Dozens."

"And why can't they help? What's wrong with them?"

"In the fictional world where we usually live, everything is logical and clear cut. Even emotional matters are logical and clear cut," Pursewarden explained. I know this sounds like a contradiction, but it is not. Just believe it for the time being; everything of an emotional nature can be analyzed rationally and becomes clear. After all, to a large extent, that's what psychologists try to accomplish."

"With some success," Irene threw in.

"Yes, but the situation is exactly the opposite in our fictional world," Pursewarden continued. "In our fictional world, everybody can analyze emotional issues and reduce them to clear cut logical understandings."

"Well, that's good, isn't it?"

"It's a big problem. It means we can't change and manipulate the emotional context of our past by thinking about it differently, which really is what psychology is about to a certain extent. Our past is clear cut, our unhappiness and suffering resulting from the past is therefore perfectly understood and clear cut, and there is just no way to deal with it emotionally on a psychological level because everything of an emotional nature is understood and clear cut."

"One should think that you can't really be unhappy in such a clear cut world," I commented.

"One should think so, but it isn't so. Everything is well understood, which is a pain, and even that pain is well understood."

"I thought we lived in a crazy world, but it seems your world is not much better."

"So what's the solution? What do you expect?" the old lady asked.

"We need to change the past. We want the past to be rewritten," Jay Gatsby replied.

"F. Scott Fitzgerald passed away in 1940," I said. "Ernest Hemingway shot himself in Ketchum in 1961, as for Lawrence Durrell, I'm not certain, but I know that he, too, is dead."

"He passed away on the 7th of November in 1990," Pursewarden pointed out.

"Thanks. What I'm driving at is this, and I believe that applies to most of you: the writers who created you are dead. They are the only ones who have the moral authority to rewrite your past. As much as I'd love to contact Fitzgerald, Hemingway, Handke, Durrell, Pamuk, Larsson, Miller, Frisch, Wallace, and whoever else your creators were, I can't. They are either dead, or they won't be interested, or I won't be interested. Not at this point in time. Maybe I won't mind talking to them at some time in the future when I'm also dead and bored. But not now."

"We're aware of this," Lady Brett Ashley replied.

"So?"

"We want you to cheat."

I thought I hadn't heard correctly and repeated what she had said. "You want me to cheat. Is that what you said?"

"That's exactly what I said."

Before I could think of something to reply, I could hear Irene yell, "At last, now we're getting somewhere!"

"Okay, we are getting somewhere," I said more to myself than to anybody else; then, returning to Brett, "What do you mean? How exactly do you want me to cheat?"

"This may be different from case to case. But take Pursewarden," she said, "in his case, we would like you to forge a document, an addendum to Durrell's will, in which Durrell stipulates that in future editions of *The Alexandria Quartet* certain changes are to be incorporated. And then, you specify the changes as per Pursewarden's wishes. The document, the paper, the ink, the handwriting, everything has to be *exactly* how it would have been if Durrell himself had written this document prior to his death. The document then has to be found somewhere where it is believable that it had gone lost and rediscovered only now. What do you think?"

"He loves it!" Irene yelled.

I looked at the old lady surprised. I didn't love it. I thought it was the craziest idea I had ever come across.

But then, suddenly, I realized I had been in this situation before. When I sat beside the old lady in a car for the very first time and she said to me: "Let's go." Once again, within less than a second, I became consciously aware of three things: she was very old, she had sparkling bright eyes, young eyes, and she displayed a charismatic beauty of a kind I had never noticed before in an elderly person.

I suspect this conscious realization triggered, in an extraordinarily quick succession, a flood of thought processes in my mind. Could this be interesting? Definitely. Is there anything more interesting I could do at present? Don't think so. Could this be dangerous? Not likely. What could go wrong? An awful lot. What would be the worst consequence if everything that could go wrong actually did? I could be accused of forgery and end up in jail (but the publicity would be fantastic). Nothing may change as far as Pursewarden is concerned. That would be bad luck for him, but he could live with it – whatever living means in his case. Easy. Decision made.

Less than a second later, I heard myself say, "Sure. Love it! Let's do it."

Now it was Pursewarden's turn to look surprised, "I didn't expect it would be that easy to convince you."

"You don't know me," I replied. I didn't know myself, but this I didn't say. "I love challenges, and this is a crazy challenge. There is really no other option but to give it a go. And besides," I remembered and said to

Pursewarden, "you saved my skin and spent a million on me, there are not many things I wouldn't be willing to do for you."

"Oh, how nice," Brett said and gave me a hug that felt more like a cuddle.

"You can repeat that any time," I commented.

"I knew I picked up the right man from the moment I saw you the first time on that crossing," the old lady said. She got up and also gave me a hug.

"Any more hugs?" I asked.

"Sure. What the heck! Why not!" Pursewarden said, and he too gave me a squeeze.

26

We agreed to make Pursewarden's case a test case. Even if we got everything right as far as the intended forgery and the distribution of the forgery were concerned, there was no guarantee that this would change his fictional fate. However, if it worked, if at the conclusion of our initiative, Pursewarden no longer remembered that he originally had committed suicide, then we could apply similar approaches to the other literary characters.

The day after the meeting with the twenty five literary characters, Pursewarden and I sat in a café in the Village and talked about how to go about what we intended to do, when a thought occurred to me, which I wondered why it hadn't occurred to me or to the old lady before. "Why,"

I asked him, "do you need me or Irene for your plan? Couldn't you just do it all by yourself? For all intents and purposes, you can do whatever I can do."

"Ah," he said, "I explained that to the old lady a few days ago. Didn't she tell you?"

"Once you are her age, and provided that you are not a never-aging literary character," I replied, "believe me, you have many other and more pressing things to worry about. I guess she just didn't think of it."

"Fair enough. I'm happy to explain it to you too."

"Go ahead."

"Literary characters, when they enter your world, can behave and act almost like human beings. The emphasis is on *almost*. We can mix with people, as you are aware, we even can influence events in the lives of human beings."

"As I'm well aware," I commented.

"Yes," he laughed, "it's amazing what one can do with money in New York."

"Not only in New York."

"However, there is one thing we can't do. We cannot take actions that would change the story of our creation. We can talk about it, we can develop ideas, we can conspire, but we cannot actually execute that last and final action or actions, which may be necessary to change the story of our creation."

"Why is that? Any idea?"

"I'm not sure, although I have a theory. But this is really nothing else but a theory."

"What is it?"

"I'm speculating that this is to prevent us from becoming God-like."

"God-like? What do you mean?"

"Well, it's like with human beings. You can't change the circumstances of your birth. If you are not happy with who you are, you can't go back and choose different parents. It's the same with us. We can do lots of stuff with our existence, but we cannot go back and change the story of our creation. If we could, we would be mightily powerful – God-like."

"I see," I replied and thought about what he had said.

After a minute, Pursewarden interrupted my thoughts by saying, "I know what you think."

"What do I think?"

"Reflecting on what we plan to do, you are asking yourself whether this doesn't mean that I'm using you. I'm trying to change the story of my creation, but since I can't do it on my own, aren't I using you – actually, misusing you – if I try to do with your help what I can't do on my own. You would also be justified in asking if I am trying to circumvent the natural laws of my literary nature with your help."

"Are you?" I asked.

"Yes I am," Pursewarden replied. "But the next question, the really important one, would have to be: is there anything wrong with this approach? If we go ahead with our plan, do we commit a crime? Do we commit a sin? Do we commit an act of wickedness?"

"Do we?"

"You have to answer this question for yourself. As far as I'm concerned, the answer is an unambiguous *no*."

"Maybe you'd better explain that to me."

"I was created by a human being, by Lawrence Durrell. This, you could say, makes him my god. You are a human being. This puts you on the same level as Lawrence Durrell. So, from my perspective, I can't see anything wrong by trying to change with the help of one god – you – something which was created a few decades ago by another god – by Lawrence."

"You should have become a lawyer," I commented with a fair bit of admiration.

"Thank you."

"But now, what about the situation I find myself in? Am I – the so called god – entitled to make changes to the creation of another so called god? Am I allowed to change what another god, a colleague of mine – Lawrence Durrell – has created? Mr. Lawyer, what's your argument in this regard?"

"Yes, definitely. From a moral perspective, you are free to do what you like. It has all happened before many times. Just look at all the changes that were made to Hemingway's manuscripts before they were published after his death."

"That's not exactly the same."

"In principle it is. There was one god who created something, even if it wasn't published during his lifetime, and then after his death, other gods arrived and rewrote it to their own desires."

"You realize you have a conflict of interest here?" I said.

"Absolutely," Pursewarden agreed.

"Nevertheless, I like your arguments concerning the ethical aspects of our plan. But what about the legal side?"

"Very simple. Firstly, if everything goes to plan, you will have committed forgery, which is a crime – so don't get caught."

"And secondly?" I asked. I was aware of the forgery aspect, but I couldn't think of what other pitfalls there could be.

"Secondly… and this is not so much a legal thing…" Pursewarden seemed to hesitate. "Well, anyhow, here it is. At some time in the future, in another world, you may meet Lawrence Durrell, and he might have something to say about what we're doing here."

"You think he might not like it?"

"There is a very real possibility, should you ever meet, that you'll meet a very unhappy man."

"Anything else?" I asked.

"I think that's it."

"Okay. I think the fun and adventure aspects of what we are planning easily override whatever concerns there may be."

"So, nothing has changed, we go ahead?"

"Nothing has changed."

27

Lawrence George Durrell died in Sommières, France, on November 7, 1990 at the age of seventy eight. That was just over two decades ago, which should make it easy, I thought, to obtain the kind of paper, ink, ballpoint pen or typewriter that he would have used if he had indeed written himself the document that we intended to forge.

Pursewarden, the old lady and I took a flight to Paris, where we stayed for two nights, and then another flight to Marseille, where we stayed for two more. We took it easy since Irene wasn't as young as she used to be, as they say. She did handle the journey extraordinarily well, though. We travelled first class and stayed in the best hotels. Pursewarden insisted that he would pay for everything, which was fair enough.

In Marseille, we rented a car. The old lady insisted on travelling in a large BMW, so a large BMW it was. Don't ask me for details. I'm not a car enthusiast. If a car gets me safely from A to B and it has climate control, I'm okay with it.

Pursewarden drove most of the time. I didn't ask him if he had a driver's license or the last time he had driven a car. I guess it could have been in England, India, or Australia. Within the first ten kilometers, he deviated several times from the right hand side of the road to the left. At a gas station, I asked him to stop. "We don't need petrol," he said. "I know," I replied, "we need something to keep you on the right side of the road."

I bought a little block of yellow self-adhesive stickers. On one sticker I penciled an arrow. Back in the car, I placed that sticker in the center of the windscreen with the arrow pointing to the right.

"Brilliant idea," Pursewarden said. Why didn't I think of that?"

Neither the old lady nor I replied. The thing that mattered was that for the rest of our journey whenever Pursewarden drove the car, which was most of the time, he stayed on the correct side of the road. He just loved driving that big BMW and was quite good at it.

Sommières is a quaint town with a Roman Bridge over the river Vidourle, a medieval center and the ruins of a castle. The river can be a bit of a problem. When it flooded in 2002, it caused major damage to the town. When we were there, it was spring, and it felt like Sommières was one of the most beautiful places in the world. I could understand that Durrell lived there for nearly a quarter of a century.

We spent four weeks in Sommières and stayed in a four and a half star hotel. The people were friendly, offering help with whatever we needed. The old lady and Pursewarden spoke French, but I only spoke English and German, and even my German is a bit rusty. Everybody in Sommières made an effort to understand me, and to make themselves understood whenever Irene or Pursewarden weren't around to interpret.

Within a week, Irene knew a dozen elderly ladies who all claimed to have known Lawrence well. Five of them said they had been his lovers. It could well be that they spoke the truth. They had handwritten letters and notes, which looked like they were at least thirty years old and which the women assured Irene were given to them by Lawrence.

Some of the letters were of considerable length, and during the second week, after the old lady had become a good friend of several of the ladies, some of them agreed that she could take a few of the lengthy letters to her hotel room and read them there at her leisure. Irene promised to return them the day after next, which she did.

One day was all Pursewarden and I needed to convince ourselves that the letters were genuine and that the paper on which the letters were written was still available in one of the local shops. The owner of the shop was a gentleman – well, a Monsieur. He was in his eighties and more than happy to chat with Pursewarden about the good old times when the Englishman was still alive. Pursewarden pointed out that he thought that Durrell wasn't really an Englishman because the English government refused to grant him a passport. "Oh, yes and no!" the shop owner said and threw his arms in the air. "Because of a technicality, they didn't give him a passport, and every time he went to London, he had to apply for a visa, but in his heart he was first of all an Englishman, then a Tibetan, then a Frenchman and a Greek."

"I guess," Pursewarden said, "he must have been one of your regular shoppers. Judging by the year when your shop was established, 1932, I believe it says above your shop window. This here was probably the only place where he could buy writing paper."

"*Exactement!*" the man replied. "Today, you can buy writing paper everywhere: in the supermarket, at the petrol station. But in the mid-1960's right through to the late 1970's this was the only place that sold stationery of any kind."

The old man closed his shop between noon and two pm, and Pursewarden invited him to lunch in a nearby restaurant. When they returned to the shop, Pursewarden knew everything he needed to know about the author who had created him. An hour later, when he left the shop, he had also in his possession twenty three items which he had bought. He only needed two, though, the writing paper, which had been forgotten in a corner of the shop's store for the past ten to fifteen years, and a pen just like the one Durrell used to write with during the last years of his life. The other items that Pursewarden bought were of no use or interest to him whatsoever. He only bought them so that the old man didn't pay any specific attention to the paper and pen. The paper and pen seemed like the least important items from an unwary observer's perspective.

Pursewarden had seen, felt, and smelled Durrell's original letters, some of which were written during the last three years of his life; he had copies of these letters. He had studied the handwriting and he had writing paper and a pen just like the one Durrell had used in Sommières. All he had to do now was to write a document – an Addendum to Lawrence Durrell's Will – and then it would be my job to make sure that that document would be discovered without resulting in an overwhelming amount of suspicion.

It was okay if the discovery of the document was perceived as mysterious, but not as suspicious.

28

The old lady went on a train journey from Nimes to Paris and then on a flight from Paris back to New York. In the event that something didn't work out as planned and Pursewarden or I, or both of us, ended up in the hands of the law, it would be better, we agreed, if Irene was in New York from where she could organize support. As far as our conspiracy was concerned, she was no longer needed, in fact, she had done her part exceptionally well.

After less than half a day of practice, Pursewarden's handwriting could not be separated from Durrell's. At first, I thought he was just an incredible talent or he had done a lot of forgery before, but Pursewarden had a more plausible explanation. Lawrence Durrell, he said, had put everything he had into the writing of *The Alexandria Quartet*. In those four books, there were two writers whom he had tailored after himself. The first one was Darley, who represented the writer Lawrence Durrell the way he saw himself: very English and rather conservative (although Darley was an Irishman). The second one was Pursewarden, who represented the writer Lawrence Durrell the way he would have liked to be. But Durrell did this only half-heartedly, perhaps lacking the courage to go all the way. One can only speculate. This may explain why he decided that Pursewarden had to commit suicide. There simply came the point when he had to go, when Durrell felt a sense of conflict within himself and no longer knew what to do with Pursewarden.

How, I asked Pursewarden, was it possible that he could forge Durrell's handwriting so perfectly that Durrell himself couldn't have done it better? He replied that a part of Durrell was within him. When Pursewarden started writing the addendum document, he slipped into Lawrence Durrell mode and was no longer Pursewarden. He hardly tried to copy Durrell's handwriting, he only had to relax and write. He felt fantastic, he admitted.

Just over two weeks after our arrival in Sommières, the document was finished and waiting for me to deposit it somewhere where it would be discovered. Already in New York, I had asked myself how to go about this part of our plan. I had discussed it with some of the literary characters, one of them was Mona, well, June. You may remember Mona is one of Henry Miller's creations and is based on his second wife, June. You may also remember that she wanted one of Henry Miller's books to be edited, well, rewritten actually. She wanted the name Mona changed to June, and she wanted Henry's exaggerations and inaccuracies to be corrected.

June reminded me that Henry Miller and Lawrence Durrell had been good friends. Almost everybody in the world of literary fiction, she said, knows about this friendship and how it had its beginning with Lawrence's letter to Henry in August 1935.

Dear Mr. Miller:

I have just read Tropic of Cancer *again and feel like I'd like to write you a line about it. It strikes me as being the only truly man-sized piece of work which this century can boast of. It's a howling triumph from the word go; and not only is it a literary and artistic smack on the bell for everyone, but it really gets down on paper the blood and bowels of our time. I have never read anything like it. I did not imagine…*

June gave me a copy of the first edition of *Tropic of Cancer*. All I needed to do, she suggested, was place the forged document in the book, and make sure that it would be discovered in a public place with lots of books. The discovery of the document would create a sensation amongst literary experts and publishers. Both together, the document and the rare book, would heighten the mystery and almost certainly create the impression that someone who had been in the possession of the book and document might have felt guilty about not revealing the existence of the document years earlier. If I liked the idea, June suggested, I could even include a little note to that extent. Something like: *Sorry folks, I forgot all about the attached addendum. A bit late now, I know. But better late than never…*

"Tell you what," she said spontaneously, "I'll write that note and I bet it won't take long, and someone will discover that it was written in my handwriting. That will create the biggest mystery in literary fiction for the past hundred years. Then, we'll only have to wait and see what happens. What do you think?"

I didn't have to think about June's suggestion twice. "That's exactly how we'll do it," I agreed and gave her a hug and a kiss. As I felt her body against mine, I understood perfectly why Henry was absolutely mad about her. But furthermore, she believed in him, and it is doubtful that he would have made it as a writer without her.

Pursewarden's addendum to Durrell's will was a short handwritten document. It stated in clear and simple English sentences, not unlike the sentences we had read in some of Durrell's letters, that after his death all future editions of his *Alexandria Quartet* books were to experience a minor revision prior to their publication. It read: *Upon reflection, I have decided that Pursewarden did not commit suicide. Suicide is foreign to his character. Although in some respect, he is a man who can be sarcastic to such an extent that he may appear non-caring which, psychologists may think, could make him a potential candidate for suicide, this shall not be the case. He is too close to my heart, and wherever there is a reference in the four books to his suicide, this reference is to be revised. The revised fictional reality is as follows: He met a Spanish woman in Greece and moved with her to Barcelona. It was there that he wrote one more novel and died soon afterwards due to injuries sustained from a car accident.*

After I had read the draft of Pursewarden's forged document, I asked him, "Why don't you let yourself die of natural causes at an old age, say in your eighties or nineties?"

"Well," he replied, "I thought of that, but that would mean that now, in my existence as a literary character, I would also have to be an old man in my eighties. Somehow, this didn't appeal to me. I think I prefer to stay around the age I am now."

"So a fictional character continues to exist at the age at which he or she appeared the last time in the book of his or her creation?" I asked.

"Yes, that's how it is most of the time, but not always," he replied. "Some literary characters continue to exist at the age that was their most prevailing age throughout the novel."

Pursewarden and I left Sommières. We stayed two days in Nice, two days in Cap Ferrat and then returned to Nice for a week. In Cape Ferrat, Somerset Maugham had spent the last decades of his life before he passed away in 1965. It had taken us nearly two weeks to make up our minds about how to make our forgery available to the world. Our original plan was to leave it in a library, but for some reason, we no longer felt comfortable with it. We decided on a different approach.

Back in Nice, dressed up as a middle aged woman and standing in front of the office of the English language newspaper, *The Riviera Times*, I gave a ten year old boy who happened to pass by an envelope and five Euro. The envelope contained a copy of the first edition of *Tropic of Cancer*, Pursewarden's forged Addendum to Durrell's Will, and the note scribbled by June. The five Euros were for the boy, but the envelope was sealed and addressed to the Editor-in-chief of *The Riviera Times*. On the back of the envelope, I had scribbled, *For publication in your paper and for circulating to Durrell's publishers. Kind regards, a friend of Durrell's.*

This approach, we concluded, would make things more mysterious than our initial library plan. Now, we had also brought one of Durrell's friends, whoever he or she might be, into the picture. The newspaper editors were told they could publish what they had received, and they were also told to make the information available to the publishers. This, we concluded, would be enough to ensure that the unexpected discovery of an addendum to Durrell's will, and the contents of the addendum, would soon be discussed in literary circles all over the world. Then, and most importantly, these discussions could lead, hopefully, to the publication of a revised edition of *The Alexandria Quartet*.

We were right, at first. *The Riviera Times* moved fast, likely because the editors wanted to ensure they got the jump on the lead, in case that someone else had received a similar envelope. When it comes to sensational or mysterious news, it is important to be the first one to report it. They published a full page feature with photos of the addendum, the book, and June's note. They either had thrown all their journalistic resources at this task, or they had an expert on everything concerning Lawrence Durrell on staff. The article discussed the addendum in the context of what was known about the last years of the writer's life which, they reasoned, made sense. This could well have been the author's final wish, although the document would have to be forensically investigated to make sure that it was not a forgery they added, just to safeguard themselves.

So far so good.

29

Pursewarden and I returned to New York. The fictitious fact that Pursewarden had not committed suicide was now in the public arena. I was wondering if perhaps this knowledge would be enough to make the literary character forget this aspect of his past, but this was not the case. Pursewarden remembered clearly that he had committed suicide.

For several weeks the media all over the western world discussed Durrell's addendum to his will. The majority of commentators were inclined to accept that it was genuine. However, where it came from and how and why it ended up on the desk of the Editor-in-chief of *The Rivera Times,* were the topics that produced the best of what modern speculative journalism had to offer. Who was the woman who had handed the envelope over to the boy together with five Euros? Why was a rare edition of one of Henry Miller's books included? Who was the author of the note that was included? Who was the author of the comment scribbled on the reverse side of the envelope? A friend? Who could that be? Were any of his friends still alive?

Did one of Henry Miller's descendants perhaps have anything to do with it?

Reading the speculative ideas and suggestions was entertaining. However, there was persistently one news item missing. Not one of the publishers of *The Alexandria Quartet* – in fact, *nobody at all* – showed any interest in doing what was now meant to be done. Those parts of the books where Durrell's suicide was mentioned were meant to be rewritten.

The man's suicide was meant to be replaced with a happier ending in Spain. At least one new edition of the four books was meant to be printed and brought to the marketplace. But nothing of the kind happened, and as far as we could tell, it wasn't even being considered. The world, the literary world, was perfectly happy with Durrell's original work. The general consensus was, if the author wanted a different fate for Pursewarden, he should have thought of it at the time of writing his major work.

After Pursewarden and I had returned from France, there was another meeting of the twenty five literary characters in the old lady's living room. Everybody was eating pizza and drinking wine and beer. We were sitting together in little groups talking about what had taken place so far. Not everybody discussed Pursewarden's case, but most of us wondered what had gone wrong.

After we had finished eating, the old lady got up and said, "There is one thing we didn't take into account."

Everybody was quiet and looked at her. After a brief pause, she said one word only: "Money."

"Money?" I could hear a few voices murmur.

"Yes, money. I should have thought of that," the old lady continued. "In today's world, nobody will do anything unless somebody pays them, or they make money off of it. Nobody rewrote the books because no one was willing to pay for it. And nobody asked for it or was willing to pay for it because none of the publishers believed that a revised edition of the books would be big business."

She sat down. No one in the room disagreed.

PART 4:

A happy ending for Lady Brett Ashley and Jake Barnes

30

For several months, little happened with the literary characters or the old lady. I had disposed of another two rapists, particularly bad ones. Reactions were frightfully positive, even the authorities and media seemed to appreciate that someone had done what the law had been unable to do. I still wasn't happy with these kinds of reactions, though. Nobody should welcome the death of a person. This may sound strange, but I'm against the death penalty. It's just that when it comes to rapists, especially the really vicious ones, my hate for these crimes makes me behave irrationally. When it comes to people's attitudes about capital punishment, I believe European countries are far ahead of those states in the USA where the death penalty is practiced.

After these last two cases, I decided to stop with my murderous part-time job, although I was honest enough to admit to myself that I could never be certain about my future actions.

Pursewarden and I went to Corfu for a week and then to Alexandria for a couple of weeks. He showed me places tourists rarely get to see, and we had a splendid time. "How is it possible," I asked him in Alexandria, "that you know these places and their histories? As far as I'm aware from Durrell's books, your name is never mentioned in the context of these locations. Even some of the locations we have been to, I believe, are not mentioned anywhere in *The Alexandria Quartet*."

"True," he replied. "I regard myself as a minor character in Durrell's work, which is quite okay with me. As far as my knowledge of these places and the history of this city are concerned, the answer is simple: I have been here as a tourist many times."

Back in New York, I finished a novel and as with another fifteen books before, I was unable to find a publisher. It didn't greatly matter, I had been an indie author (self-published author) for nearly fifteen years. I wrote, produced, and sold my books, all by myself.

Until a few years ago, I had printed and sold my books. The day that all changed was when I received an email: *"Hello, We are excited to announce Kindle Direct Publishing..."*

At first I ignored it. That I was looking at a business opportunity of a kind that does not present itself very often in life, did not click with me at first. The world of eBooks had arrived and was waiting to be conquered.

One day I read the email more thoroughly, opened the links, and studied the Amazon Kindle Direct Publishing web pages. Four days later, my first eBook was one of the books in the Kindle store. A few weeks later, all of my books were available as Kindle eBooks.

One evening, as I was reflecting on eBooks and literary characters in the old lady's living room, a new idea emerged. I asked Jay to edit *The Great Gatsby*. "Edit it. Rewrite it. Produce exactly the book that you want and that you are going to be happy with."

To enable him to do this as efficiently as possible, June and I had arranged for the pages of the book to be run through an OCR scanner in a printer's workshop in Brooklyn. An OCR scanner is a machine that converts the words on the book's paper pages into electronic files, in this case, into Word for Windows files. The book can then be edited with a PC. It turned out that Jay Gatsby was reasonably computer literate, which came as a surprise to me. Just as Pursewarden had done a lot of travelling, Jay had done a lot of studying and had acquired skills in working with Microsoft Word.

After two weeks of editing, Jay showed me the result of his work: a printout of the revised *Great Gatsby*. All the changes he had made were in red, the text that he hadn't touched was in black. I was surprised; there weren't too many changes, probably five per cent of the book was affected. The ending was different of course. Instead of Jay floating dead in a swimming pool, it was now the man who had shot at him, Wilson, who was floating dead in the pool. But Wilson had not turned the gun onto himself as he had done in the original version. Instead, he was shot by Gatsby's gardener after Wilson had shot at Gatsby but missed. That was a real surprise and I liked it. Gatsby then arranged a great funeral for Wilson, which was an even bigger surprise.

However, Jay's English wasn't nearly as good as F. Scott Fitzgerald's. "Go and talk to Hemingway," I told him. "He should be able to correct your grammar and improve your style. It's important that the changes you made melt into Scott's writing."

When a month later I still hadn't heard from him, I asked one of the other literary characters, who was hanging around in the living room, to contact Jay and ask him to see me. An hour later, he turned up. He didn't look happy. "Hemingway," he complained, "is rewriting the entire book. There is hardly a sentence in the book that he's happy with."

Oh, no, I thought, I should have anticipated that. "Never mind," I said, "let Hemingway do what he thinks has to be done. It'll probably take him a year or longer to finish that job. He's too much of a perfectionist. Print another copy of the book and give it to Pursewarden and ask him to knock it into shape. His English is pretty good."

A few days later, Jay returned with the revised book and when I read the parts he and Pursewarden had rewritten, I was awe-struck. I think F. Scott Fitzgerald would have been impressed too. Whether he would have approved the plot of the new version of his work is an entirely different question.

A few weeks earlier, Lisbeth Salander, who was a genius computer hacker, told me about a real life computer hacker. His name was Geoff and he lived in Harlem. She had met him a few years ago and told me that every now and then they end up together for a few days. She said it was only when either of them were lonely. I thought that was a sensible way of dealing with loneliness.

"I know how you can get in touch with him when you are lonely," I had said at the time. "You simply turn up. But how does he get in touch with you when he feels lonely? He can't just turn up in your fictional world."

"No he can't," Lisbeth had agreed, "but he can send me an email."

"You are joking! He can't send an email from real life Harlem to the fictional world of *The Girl With The Dragon Tattoo*, or can he?"

"He can," she replied. "He is the only one who can; he is the best hacker in New York, perhaps the best in America."

To me, this sounded a bit like sending an email from Planet Earth to God in Heaven. "Amazing!" I was practically speechless.

I asked Jay to contact Lisbeth and ask her, if possible, to see me together with Geoff. Twenty minutes later Lisbeth was in Irene's living room; another twenty minutes later the entrance doorbell rang and Geoff arrived by taxi from Harlem. She must have sent an email from her world to his world. I didn't ask. Geoff's appearance was how I had expected him to be: black, overweight, and meticulously dressed in a black suit, a colorful T-shirt, and white gel Asics. I don't know why I had this picture of him. Spooky, if you ask me. Geoff introduced himself and told me, as far as computers, programming, software, and hacking were concerned, if something could be done, he could do it. He said, "I can't make a computer fly, but I can hack into every airline's computer system and bring every plane down to earth."

"Heck," I said, "that's the last thing I want you to do."

"It's just an example," he replied.

I explained to him what Jay, June, and I had in mind. I asked him to break into an online book retail computer system that had electronic copies of *The Great Gatsby* stored, and replace the existing copies with revised ones. "There shouldn't be too many," I pointed out. "First of all, of course, there is Amazon, then there are a few publishers."

"What about the readers?" Geoff interrupted me.

"Well, there are probably thousands of people who have downloaded the book to their Kindles, iPads and eReaders, but I don't expect you to break into thousands of individual eBook Readers."

"Don't worry. I can do that with a few lines of code."

"How?" June asked.

Geoff looked at her and I could see what went through his mind. "If I explain that to you, will you understand it?" he said rhetorically. "Okay," he then said, "once I'm inside Amazon's computer system, I can locate, probably in one of their financial systems, the files that contain the email addresses and other info about every person that has downloaded *The Great Gatsby*."

"Understood," June interrupted him.

"You sure?"

"Of course. The rest is simple. You write a little program, a virus actually, you hide that program somewhere in Amazon's gigantic system world, and whenever your program is activated, it flashes it's instructions through cyberspace and replaces within seconds thousands of existing versions of *The Great Gatsby* with the revised version."

"Very good!" Geoff looked at her, and I could see he was impressed.

"When do you want to start?" I asked Geoff.

"When do you want me to start?"

"Any time you like. You can start now if you like." I didn't actually mean it; I just wanted to make it clear that everything was ready.

"Okay. Can I use your notebook?"

"We bought you a new one," I answered, "with a separate wireless connection and all sorts of safety features to make sure nobody can trace what you're doing back here."

"Don't worry, I'll install my own kill-trace safety features."

"Kill-trace... Sounds good."

I gave him a brand new and super powerful notebook computer. Jay gave him a USB stick that contained a copy of the new version of *The Great Gatsby*. Geoff went to a table in a corner area and from there he said, "There are a few more things I need."

"What is it?" June asked.

"A cold beer, a strong coffee, bourbon, and a sandwich every hour. Just talk to Lisbeth, she knows what kind of stuff I prefer. She'll probably be happy to hang around while I'm here."

"No problem."

31

When Lisbeth popped in a bit later, just before midnight, I asked her, "Would you like to show Geoff where the guest room's located? Or is he going back to Harlem when he's tired?"

"I think he'll work through the night and finish some time tomorrow."

"Really?"

"Yes! That's how he functions. Just as Stieg Larsson lived in a different world when he sat in front of his PC and wrote his novels, Geoff lives in a different world when he's doing what he enjoys most – journeying through other people's computer systems."

"These crazy working hours together with the stuff he wants every hour will kill him."

"To the contrary, it'll keep him alive. Don't worry. I'll stay up and make sure he has what he needs."

"Okay… Well… Good night," I said and went to my quarters. Ten minutes later, I was asleep. The time was half past midnight.

I woke up at six am and fell asleep again. When I awoke for the second time, it was half past nine. I felt refreshed, brushed my teeth, had an almost cold shower, and was looking forward to a great breakfast.

Lisbeth and June were sleeping together on one of the three sofas in the living room. I could see there were two girls, young women really, who had become friends. I was happy for them.

Geoff was sitting in the corner of the room in front of the notebook computer. He was hammering away on the keyboard as if there was no tomorrow. There were empty beer bottles on the floor, all nicely lined up along the wall.

"How're things?" I asked.

Geoff didn't reply. I could see his mind was elsewhere.

I went to the kitchen. Sue was in the process of preparing my breakfast. I had left a note for her the evening before, asking for the unhealthiest and most delicious breakfast she could think of.

She exceeded my expectations. I spent nearly an hour in the kitchen eating, chatting with Sue, reading *The New York Times,* and watching CNN business news. Life was great.

I asked Sue if she had heard anything from Irene.

"We talked on Skype an hour ago," she said.

"Is everything all right?"

"Oh yes, she said she'll do that cruise again next year."

"She's crazy," I mumbled.

Sue didn't reply. She knew that I didn't really mean it, but she also agreed that there was some truth in my comment. The old lady was on a cruise somewhere up north between Canada and Greenland and wasn't due back for another two weeks. I had no idea what attracted her to that part of the world. It was cold, dangerous, boring, and as far as I was concerned, that was it. But that's just me. I'm a city person. If I want to experience nature, I go for an hour into Central Park.

If I had known that by the time of her return her apartment would no longer be inhabitable, that it would have turned into a burned out shell, I'd probably have said YES when she asked me two months ago if I'd like to come along.

Pursewarden, Jay, and I went to an early dinner at a restaurant in the neighborhood at around six pm. Geoff was still working in front of the notebook computer. I don't think I've ever seen a man more focused than he. Sometimes, he'd just sit and stare at the monitor for ten to twenty minutes, then he'd suddenly jump into action and worked the keyboard at an incredible speed.

June and Lisbeth were in the living room. June looked amazingly fresh, relaxed, and as always, very beautiful. At regular intervals, Lisbeth provided Geoff with coffee and cake.

"No more sandwiches, no more beer?" I asked before we left.

"I think Amazon's firewall and system security features are giving him a hell of a hard time," Lisbeth replied. "He's now on a high sugar diet which converts quickly into energy."

"Tell him to have a break," Jay said.

"He'll happily have a break when he's finished," she replied.

When we returned from dinner two hours later, Geoff, Lisbeth and June were gone. I went to my notebook computer and accessed my Amazon account. A minute later, I downloaded an electronic version of *The Great Gatsby* into my Kindle. I gave the Kindle to Pursewarden and asked him to check if the book was the old or the revised version. It didn't take long, and he said, "That son of a gun did it."

In roughly twenty four hours, Geoff had converted close to one hundred per cent of all eBook versions of *The Great Gatsby* in the world into the new version in which Jay Gatsby at the end of the book was still alive.

Jay, who had been in the kitchen returned with three bottles of beer. "How're you feeling?" I asked him.

"Good. Why do you ask?"

"Just wondering."

"Has anything happened?" he asked slightly suspicious.

"Geoff's finished his job," Pursewarden said.

Jay look towards the corner where Geoff had been working and asked, "What job?"

"Your job."

"Did I give him a job?"

"Yes, you did. Don't you remember?" I asked.

"No. But whatever it was, I'm glad he finished it."

Pursewarden looked at me, and I looked at him and we each were thinking the same. Who is going to tell Jay what this was all about?

Pursewarden started, "You remember you are a literary character that was created in the 1920's by F. Scott Fitzgerald?"

"Sure," Jay answered. "I don't suffer from amnesia. Why do you ask?"

"How did the book end?"

"*The Great Gatsby*, I assume you are talking about?"

"Yes," I confirmed. "*The Great Gatsby*. How did the novel end?"

"Daisy divorced Tom and married me. Poor Wilson was shot and left dead in the swimming pool. He had a well-attended funeral. Daisy and I went to Mexico. But you know that. Why do you ask?"

"Holy shit!" I heard Pursewarden saying. "It worked! It really worked!"

We spent an hour trying to explain to Jay Gatsby what we were talking about, that he had rewritten the famous book, but he thought we were joking. He remembered nothing. He refused to believe a word of what we said. He was a new Jay Gatsby, exactly the way it had been planned by him and was meant to be.

There was only one thing I was worried about. What would happen when he returned to the old paper version of *The Great Gatsby* in the library?

32

I found out a few hours later, when Jay *did* return to the library. It took less than five minutes and he was back in the living room and complained about headaches, nausea and depression. "Never felt that bad in my life," he said. But then, within another five minutes, he felt all right again.

"You can't go back to that old book," I said. "In the old book, you are the one who is floating dead in the swimming pool, which is contrary to your new understanding of yourself, and that creates a massive conflict within yourself."

Before I could continue, he interrupted me. "Please, stop making that stupid joke."

"I'm afraid it's not a joke."

But as before, he didn't believe and ten minutes later went back to the library. "Must have been a one off thing," he said. "I'm feeling great now. Maybe it was something I've eaten in the restaurant."

Five minutes later he was back. He looked pale and worried. "Could you do me a favor?" he asked. "Go to the library, fetch the book and see if you can find the page where it supposedly says that I'm floating dead in the swimming pool."

"Good idea," I replied and returned a minute later with the book. It took me a while to find the page I was looking for. I read the relevant paragraph to him. He took the book and read the entire page himself.

When he finished, he placed the book on the coffee table in front of us and said, "I can't go back into this book."

I agreed. "This book is no longer your home."

I poured us two triple bourbons. For a while, we were just sitting there in silence.

Whiskey, it seemed, stimulated my thoughts. I had a sudden idea and asked him, "Could you live in an electronic version of the new book?" I showed him my Kindle and told him that it contained the new version of *The Great Gatsby*. He took the Kindle and I showed him how to find the book and how to operate the Kindle. He paged almost through to the end of the book when he found and read to me that the dead man in the swimming pool was Wilson. At least now, he was convinced that there were two versions of *The Great Gatsby* in existence.

"Let me take that Kindle to the library," he said after a while. "Right here I can't see how I could move into another reality, but maybe in the library I can think of something. The library always seemed to me like an in-between world, a world that's neither one hundred per cent real nor one hundred per cent fiction."

When he hadn't returned after twenty minutes I followed him. I half expected to find my Kindle somewhere but Jay Gatsby nowhere, and was already wondering how it might feel to walk with a Kindle around knowing that it was the home of someone I knew personally. But that was not meant to be, although it would have solved a problem beautifully.

Jay was sitting on a chair with my Kindle on a table in front of him. He looked at that little computer, which is all a Kindle really is. When he noticed me coming in, he shook his head and said, "Thinking about how I might be able to get inside that thing makes me feel like an idiot," he said.

"Would be the same with me," I commented. "Come, let's have another glass of bourbon before we go to bed. You can sleep in one of the guest rooms tonight."

The next morning at the breakfast table, June and Pursewarden joined us. Jay told them what had happened last night. We talked about it and tossed ideas around when suddenly, out of the blue, June said, "We need a printed version of the new edition of the book in the library and the old version can go into a rubbish bin or storage room."

I could see that Jay and Pursewarden were thinking exactly what I thought: why the heck didn't we think of that? There was nothing male or chauvinistic in that question. Simply the fact that this was such an obvious thing to try and that none of us had thought of it was what irked us.

We went to the printing company in Brooklyn and asked the owner to produce two hard cover copies of the new version of *The Great Gatsby*.

Jay gave him the USB stick with the file of the book. I said, "We need the books by tomorrow, lunch time." Pursewarden took two thousand dollars from one of his trouser pockets and gave them to the man and said, "This is a deposit. Tomorrow at lunch time, you will receive the same again as final payment."

"That's okay," the man said. "No final payment needed. See you tomorrow at twelve noon."

"A good and honest New Yorker," I said on the way home. "He is willing to take a bit extra, but then there is a line somewhere, which he is not willing to cross."

"Didn't know such people existed," Pursewarden said, and it sounded slightly sarcastic, just the way I remembered him from *The Alexandria Quartet*.

"There are probably many like him," I added, "you just don't meet them that often."

"You mean because I mix with the wrong crowd?"

"Not right now," Jay laughed. "Right now, you are with the good crowd."

"How about a second breakfast somewhere?" June suggested.

Everybody thought that was a good idea.

Jay spent another night in the guest room. The next morning, the four of us had breakfast together again. We talked about all sorts of things except the two books that we were going to pick up at lunchtime. Jay seemed nervous and asked for a glass of bourbon. I said, "You know where the stuff's located. Just help yourself." After he had his drink, he seemed more relaxed.

"Don't worry," June said to him. "If it comes to the worst and you can never return to your fictional existence, life here in New York isn't that bad either. I grew up here."

"Is that the best you can do to cheer me up?" Jay asked. He seemed confused, as if he were dealing with some sort of conflict within himself.

"I thought that was pretty good," June replied.

At around eleven am, we went to the same place where we had had our second breakfast the day before. All of us, except Jay, ordered something to eat. Jay limited himself to a cup of coffee.

At twelve noon, we arrived at the printer's office and were handed over two good-looking hard cover copies of the new and latest printed edition of *The Great Gatsby*. "What would Fitzgerald say?" June asked.

"He'd probably hate it," Pursewarden answered.

"What are you talking about?" Jay asked.

"Never mind, never mind," I remarked. "Now that we've committed the literary crime of the century and published a revised version of *The Great Gatsby*, both in eBook and now also in print format, let us hope that our crime pays off and that Jay will find access to his old world in the library once more."

"Hear, hear," Pursewarden mumbled.

"Do you have to be so terribly English?" June asked.

"Yes, I have to."

"Why?"

"Because that's how it's written."

"Where?"

"In the book of the future."

"Are you saying there is a book in which everything that's going to happen in the future is recorded already today?"

Oh no! I thought, that's a very heavy philosophical topic. Not now.

"That's what I'm saying," Pursewarden replied.

"Nonsense!" June decided after a moment of thought. "That would take all the fun away from what we are doing." After a few more moments, she continued, "Even if there were such a book, and even if it were in the library, I'd suggest that we just pretend that there isn't such a book."

"Okay," Pursewarden agreed, "but you realize of course that your decision to pretend that there isn't such a book is also predetermined and recorded in the book."

"I don't like this book. I don't like this damn book one bit," June concluded the conversation.

Nobody would like it, I thought, but its existence – the possibility that everything is predetermined – is a very real possibility. Even Stephen Hawking thinks it is.

When we arrived at the old lady's place, which I called home by now, Jay went straight into the library. He had one copy of the new edition of *The Great Gatsby* with him. He returned from the library less than a minute later and handed me the old edition of the book. "Hide it. Far away," he said, and went straight back into the library.

He didn't return until the next morning for breakfast. "How're you doing today?" I asked.

"Couldn't be better," he replied.

"So you had a good night's sleep?"

"Sure had."

"So everything's fine?"

"Why wouldn't it be?"

"Just wondering."

As it turned out, he couldn't remember a thing about what had happened the previous two days when he found himself in limbo. As far as Jay Gatsby was concerned, he had never floated dead in a swimming pool. Since that day decades ago when the first copy of *The Great Gatsby* left the printing press, the dead man floating in the swimming pool had been Wilson.

"Well," I said, "we have the blueprint now for making a few more literary characters just as happy as you."

"What are you talking about?"

"Never mind. I'll tell you another time."

"Why not now?

"Because you wouldn't believe me."

33

For the next evening, I called a meeting of all the literary characters who'd like to have something changed in the books, in which they commenced their journeys. I knew that by now, every literary character in all the books in the old lady's library knew about the events of the past weeks: about our failed attempt to have Pursewarden's history rewritten and about the challenges and what was involved to successfully change Jay Gatsby's past without preventing him from returning to his fictional world.

There were thousands of literary characters in the books in the library: very famous ones and minor ones. I had decided to allow every one of them to come forward; accordingly, I expected a full house – at least hundreds of them – and I was wondering what I would do in the event that Irene's huge apartment was too small for that meeting.

To my surprise, only the same twenty five literary characters turned up that had participated from the beginning, that was when Pursewarden wrote an addendum to Durrell's will. "How did you prevent the others from coming?" I asked. "Did you tell them horror stories about your experiences?" I looked at Jay, Pursewarden and June.

"No," June replied. "Everything was objectively explained on TV and everybody was invited to participate if they so wished."

"Initially," I said, "going back to the time when I had just moved into this apartment, there were nearly two hundred of you in this room and I thought they all wanted parts of their past erased and rewritten. What happened to them?"

"I think," an old man said, "many were just inquisitive."

"Okay," I agreed. "But please tell me again, who are you? I know we met before, but I can't remember…"

"I'm Allan Karlsson from…"

"*The 100-Year-Old Man Who Climbed Out the Window and Disappeared*," I finished his sentence.

"That's me," the old man confirmed.

"I remember; you want to fix a few translation problems. Nothing else, I hope. The book as it is now is just perfect. One of the most entertaining novels on the market."

"I agree. However, and I thought long and hard about this, there is one substantial change I would like to make. You see, the problem is my age. I don't want to be one hundred."

"How old would you like to be?"

"How about eighty?"

"Well that's not a problem for me," I replied, "but that will make quite a difference to the book. Even the book's title will no longer be the same."

"I don't think that's a problem," the old man replied.

"Okay, but it would be a problem to Jonas Jonasson and the rest of the world, and by that I mean it will be a problem for many people living in the real world."

"Everything we do here will be a problem for many people living in the real world."

He was right. I expected to read something about the revised eBook version of *The Great Gatsby* in *The New York Times* every day. I said, "So you think you could just as well make yourself twenty years younger?"

"Sure!"

"Okay." I laughed. "I'm with you." I couldn't help myself. What we were doing seemed so very, very crazy.

It was agreed that I should chair the meeting. "You called it, why don't you chair it?" Pursewarden said, and everybody muttered something which sounded like consent.

I started by saying, "Now that we know what has to be done, I suggest we put all our resources and every effort into getting this initiative completed within one week, sooner if possible."

"What's the hurry?" someone asked.

"I expect within the next twenty four to forty eight hours, someone will discover the revised eBook versions of *The Great Gatsby*. I don't expect that Amazon will find anything in their systems environment that shows that their environment had been hacked into. Geoff, I was told, is too good at what he does. However, the Engineers at Amazon will conclude, probably rather sooner than later, that they were, indeed, under attack by a hacker. This will mean they will add additional firewalls and protective features to their computers. Ideally, I would like to see our initiative completed before Amazon starts implementing major security upgrades."

"To get all we have to do done in just one week, is that feasible?" June asked.

"It is," I replied. "I have a plan and that plan means a lot of work.

"Shoot," Jack Reacher said.

I pretended to pull a gun and aimed at him. He did the same, aiming at me. I think he was faster by a fraction of a second; he probably had more practice. Putting my imaginary gun back into my pocket, I continued. "Tomorrow morning, at nine o'clock, we all go to the printing company in Brooklyn. Please take with you the book that you want to edit or rewrite. At the company, all books will be OCR read and stored in Word for Windows format on a USB stick; one USB stick for each book. To do an OCR read of one book takes about ten minutes. The company has the most sophisticated equipment available for that job, the book does not have to be damaged and the boss and everybody working there know that we will be coming and they will give high priority to our projects. As soon as you have the USB stick containing the file of your book, grab a taxi and return with the printed version of your book and the USB stick to this apartment.

"But before tomorrow, there is tonight. When we have finished this meeting, I want you to return to your world and get in touch with characters who can help you to edit and rewrite your book the way you want it. When you return from the printer tomorrow with your USB stick and go back to your literary world, it is important that you have lined up whatever help and resources you need to edit and rewrite your book.

"For those of you who are computer literate and possess a good command of the language in which your book is written, this could mean that all you need is a PC with Word for Windows installed, and you can go ahead and do what you have to do. For those of you who have never touched a computer keyboard and are struggling to write meaningful sentences, you may need the assistance of a writer or a professional editor and the help of someone who is good with computers.

"Whatever assistance and resources you need, line them up tonight so that tomorrow, when you return from the printer, you can start editing and rewriting the book right away. If any of you are confused and have no idea what I'm talking about, talk to June or Pursewarden. Either of them can connect you with the right people in your world. Pursewarden will also provide you with enough money for the taxi tomorrow, and for a quick meal if you feel like having a bite while you are out there. As long as you don't fall foul of the law and get caught by the police, all will be fine.

"Some of you want to make minor modifications to the book that started your existence, like Jack Reacher, he wants to change only one sentence; but some of you, as I understand it, want to rewrite major parts of the book. Accordingly, I expect some of you to have completed your job tomorrow within a couple of hours, for others it may take a couple of days. Whenever the job you are doing is finished – but please, please make sure that the changes you make to the book are thoroughly edited – return to this apartment with the USB stick which contains the file of the revised version of the book.

"Geoff will be here. Give him your USB stick, and he will copy the file of the book from the stick to the Notebook computer in the corner over there. This will take a minute or two. In the meantime, I'll have a taxi organized that'll take you to the printing factory in Brooklyn. Give the USB stick to the boss, his name is George Drucker. He will know what to do. Don't chat with him. We want him to get on with the job of printing two hard cover copies of your book without delay. With a bit of luck, we should have the printed version of the book back within twenty four hours. George will return all books by courier.

"While you're at the printer's, Geoff will reformat the file of your book, so that it is suitable for publication as an eBook. Actually, he has a smart program that will do that job for him.

"He will place the files of all the books that are ready for eBook publication in a queue in his computer, waiting to be sent into cyberspace with one mouse click to find their ways to Amazon, Barnes and Noble, Smashwords and other eBook retailers. When he has all twenty five files from you, he will release the files at once.

"We thought about the release of the files quite a bit. Geoff could release each file individually, but inherent in this approach would be the risk that firms like Amazon could notice that something funny is going on and shut down parts of their computer systems that we need access to. If they shut down these systems before we have transferred all twenty five files, some of the revisions would be left out in the cold. It's better to hack into their system once only, and then sit back, and see what happens.

"I think that's pretty much it. I'm sure I've forgotten a few things or some of what I said didn't make much sense to some of you, so please ask questions now, and I'll do my best to answer them."

There weren't many questions, and they were easily answered. It seemed that I had done a passable job of explaining the plan. I noticed about half a dozen literary characters walked straight to June and Pursewarden to discuss details about the resources and the assistance they had to organize during the night ahead.

34

Amazingly, six days later, all the twenty five revised and rewritten books were sitting in a queue in Geoff's computer, waiting to be released. *The Bible* was not amongst them. Just as Jesus had told us earlier, to change this book into a more suspenseful and humorous book was a major task, which would take several years.

June was the last one to have her work submitted. I knew she appeared as Mona in quite a few of her former husband's books, and I had asked her earlier if she wanted to edit and rewrite all the books in which she appeared or what her intentions were. She answered there was only one book she wanted to get right: that book was *Sexus*.

Sexus, she told me, was emotionally closest to her heart. Initially, she had intended to rewrite *Tropic of Cancer*, but had changed her mind. I had read *Sexus* years earlier and liked it. I have to add, I like most of Henry Miller's books, but not primarily because of the sex scenes in some of them. I like his books because they are unashamedly positive. Even in his miserable and difficult early years in New York and later in Paris, Henry always found something to be excited about.

I asked June how much of the book she had rewritten. "Quite a lot!" she replied.

"How much?" She looked at me, smiled and said, "The name of the author should now read June Miller." I must have looked a bit shocked. She quickly added, "Don't worry, it still says Henry Miller on the title page."

"Well," I said, looking to Geoff, "are you ready to push the release button?"

"Sure am," he replied.

There were twenty seven of us in the living room, or maybe that should read: two people – Geoff and I – and twenty five literary characters. We started to count down from ten to zero. At zero Geoff released with a mouse click twenty five books into cyberspace. We live in an amazing world, I thought. We can send books with the speed of light to any place on the globe, and nobody seems to think that this is something special. Maybe to have a bunch of literary characters in one's living room will be the same matter of course in another ten or twenty years' time.

Earlier in the day, Pursewarden had organized the delivery of three dozen of the best bottles of French champagne he could locate in New York. For the next couple of hours, the corks were popping and we were celebrating. When I asked Brett Ashley how Jake was doing, she replied that she and Jake were happily married. They now had a son and a daughter and Jake was looking after them during the celebration. Once more I thought, this is an utterly amazing world. The original Jake Barnes in *The Sun Also Rises* was impotent; now the same man is happily married to the woman he loves and they have two children. I asked Brett if Jake had been impotent at one stage. "Not sure what you are talking about," she replied, and I could see that she didn't think this was a good joke. "Sorry," I said, "I think I confused Jake with another character in another book." "No big deal," she replied, "it can happen to anybody."

At the end of the celebration, there was only one more task to be done. Twenty five old and obsolete books had to be replaced in the library with twenty five new and revised ones. The old versions ended up in the storage room. Of each of the new books we had two hard cover copies. One copy went into the library and the other copy in a book shelf in my quarters.

A few days later, I discovered that already by the time we had finished our celebration, of each of the twenty five revised eBooks between 100,000 and 1,000,000 copies were downloaded into Kindles and other eBook Readers by people all over the planet. Geoff, with his infinite hacking wisdom, had not only replaced old eBook versions with new ones at places like Amazon, Barnes and Nobles, and Smashwords, he had also changed the price of the new versions to $0.00, and he had broadcasted this exciting news to every person with a Facebook and Twitter account.

The next day all hell broke loose.

PART 5:

The unanimous decision of the philosophy aficionados

35

I woke up at five am. There was a fracas coming from the living room and entryway of the apartment. I got up to check out what was going on and stumbled upon a living room full of people. I was still half asleep, and it took me a while to work out that most of the figures that I thought were people were literary characters: exactly twenty five as I found out later. But there were also real people – about half a dozen police officers – many of them overweight. This reminded me that I wanted to join a fitness club.

One of the police officers spotted me and pointed towards me. He yelled something, and with his gun in his hand, tried to push his way towards me. He was stopped by a handful of the literary characters. Now another police officer spotted me. And another one... And another one... They all failed. The literary characters had formed a wall between me and the police, and not one police officer managed to get through to me.

Two shots were fired into the ceiling of the living room. At first I thought they were fired by the police, but Jack Reacher was the one to blame, as I was told later. For the police, this was the sign to join in. Some shot at the ceiling, one Police officer shot a bullet into the wall behind me, missing my head by two inches. I wondered if that was intentional or if he was just a bad shot. If the latter was the case, they should train him better or give him an office job. Nonetheless, I was glad he had missed.

The next shot, from another police officer, didn't miss. Well, he didn't miss entirely. The bullet grazed the left side of my head, just about half an inch above my ear and an eighth of an inch deep. A little deeper and my brain would have been visible.

For the next one and a half weeks I was unconscious. As I was told later, the twenty five literary characters had managed to overwhelm the police officers, amazingly without anybody being killed. During the fight, Pursewarden and June had managed to get me out of the building, into a taxi and to a small hospital in Brooklyn. Apparently, Pursewarden had told the taxi driver, "This man needs to go to a good doctor where the police can't find him." He gave the driver one thousand dollars, and the man took him, June, and me to a five bed hospital that was disguised as a Prayer Center and unknown to almost everyone in New York. The taxi driver stopped a few houses away from the place and said to Pursewarden, "You have to carry him the last few yards; I don't want my taxi to be seen. Take him straight into the house. They will tell you to leave. I suggest you make a big fuss, offer them big money, tell them that the police are after you. Don't tell them who brought you here. Okay?"

"Okay," Pursewarden agreed, and half an hour later, after Pursewarden was nearly shot at by one of the gangsters in the house, a doctor agreed to look at me. He said to June, "He'll either live or die."

"In this case," June replied, "he'll live." She was right, but it took a bit over a week for me to regain consciousness. The doctor was a bit baffled by this because the injury wasn't that bad. My skull had a deep scratch, but that was only damage to the bone. "The bullet must have shaken his brain a bit," was the only explanation the doctor could offer.

During the fight between the literary characters and the police, a fire had broken out in the apartment. Someone had fired a bullet first into a half full bottle of whiskey that was standing beside Geoff's notebook computer. A few seconds later, either the same person or someone else, had fired a bullet into Geoff's notebook. One theory is that this could have created a spark and the spark could have ignited the Whiskey. There is another theory: that one of the police officers lit the fire deliberately. But I find that hard to believe. Police officers wouldn't do such a thing – would they?

Whichever way it may have happened, the fire spread quickly and destroyed the entire apartment including the library. Fortunately it didn't take long for the fire fighters to arrive. They managed to rescue the building and keep the damage to the neighboring apartments to a minimum.

The remaining twenty three literary characters (remember, Pursewarden and June had escaped a few minutes earlier and taken me to the hospital) and the police managed to get out of the building, some with abrasions, bruises, and black eyes. Outside the building, what seemed like half of New York's police force was waiting for them. That's how Jack Reacher remembered it. The twenty three literary characters were arrested.

36

By the time I had regained consciousness, the old lady had returned from her cruise. June picked her up from the port and told her what had happened. Irene wasn't worried about the apartment, it was well insured she pointed out. She was worried about me and the twenty three literary characters in jail.

June told her that I would be out of the gangsters' hospital – that's what she called it – within a day or two. It had cost Pursewarden a six digit figure to pay for me to receive treatment there, though. He didn't mind. But the first thing he did after the hospital had given in and agreed to treat me, he bought himself and June a gun. He also made sure that either he or June were always with me in my room. These two – and I hope you don't mind if I call them *people* for a change – these two *people* and the old lady had become my best friends.

When I left the hospital, we knew close to nothing about the twenty three literary characters in jail. They had no identification, and likely didn't exactly know why they were in prison in the first place. Their fight with the police hadn't been a big calamity, any halfway decent lawyer should have managed to bail them out within a couple of days. Although, I suppose, they must have appeared to the authorities as a rather mysterious group of people.

After their release, they told me that they had decided to stick to the truth. They told the interrogating officers their real names and that they were literary characters. Of course, nobody believed them. Even after each of them was questioned whilst connected to a lie detector, with results confirming that they spoke the truth, nobody believed them. When a police woman asked Jay Gatsby how the book, *The Great Gatsby*, ended, and he told her that he, of course, had married Daisy and they went to Mexico, and the dead man who floated in the swimming pool was Wilson, that was the moment when there was little doubt any longer in the thinking of the police interrogators that they were dealing with a bunch of crazy imposters. When they did the same test, I guess you could call it a *literary test*, with the other literary characters and each one of them told them a version of the novel from which they had originated, a version that was not in accordance with the original, it was overwhelmingly clear to the interrogators that they were dealing with a bunch of liars. But why, the police wondered, why would twenty three people come up with such crazy stories? There must be a major conspiracy behind all this, they concluded.

The shit hit the fan, well and truly, when the media all over the world reported that new versions – all of them eBook versions – of famous books like *The Great Gatsby, Sexus, The Alexandria Quartet,* and *The Old Man and the Sea* had appeared at Amazon and other online book stores. Now, at least for a few hours, everything seemed to make sense to the detectives. These people were trying to make money by hacking into online book stores and publishing new, absurd versions of famous books.

There was just one problem: there was no money involved. The millions of books that were sold, were sold for $0.00.

37

The day after the old lady's return from her cruise holiday and after my release from hospital, she, June, Pursewarden, and I went to her lawyer. We were less than two minutes in the man's office when the door opened and the Lincoln Lawyer walked in.

"Amazing what you guys have done!" he yelled before he said hi. "I've heard all about it on TV this morning. As of an hour ago, they've discovered fourteen modified books. How many did you do altogether?"

"Twenty five," Pursewarden replied, "but it wasn't just us who did it, it was us and twenty three of our friends who are in prison now."

"I see. And that's why you are here."

"Exactly. We have to get them out."

"Have they killed anybody?" he asked.

"Not in this world," I replied. "Some of them, like Jack Reacher, have done a lot of killings in their literary world."

"Jack's with them! This case is getting better every minute." The man looked very happy. "Literary killings, by the way, don't count. But they, and probably you, need a lawyer. I'd be happy to take on this case."

"You're hired!" June said.

"There is one condition."

"Money?" Pursewarden asked.

"Not money. I've all the money I need. When it's all over I want you to help me edit and publish a revised version of the book I'm in."

"I'm sure that can be done," I replied. "By then Amazon and the other online retailers will probably have installed more sophisticated and protective features around their systems. But I'm confident that our IT guru, Geoff, will find a way to figure it out."

It was at that point that the old lady's lawyer added something to the conversation. So far, he had just listened and I could see that the case the Lincoln Lawyer was about to take on fascinated him just as much as everybody else. Turning towards the literary lawyer he said, "You need to be licensed to practice law in the State of New York. At this stage, you aren't registered anywhere in the United States, you don't even exist."

"Good point," replied the lawyer who didn't exist. "From now on, please don't call me the Lincoln Lawyer and also don't refer to me by my real name Mickey Haller. Allow me to introduce myself, my name is Matthew McConaughey, and I'm a registered criminal defense attorney in the City of New York. Since you are my friends, please call me Matt."

"How did you manage that?" the old lady's lawyer asked.

"That I can't tell you. I'm not willing to incriminate myself."

"Fair enough, but tell me, how much do you really know about the law?"

"Everything Michael Connelly taught me."

"In other words, not enough. You need a partner." Looking towards Pursewarden and the old lady he added, "My normal fee applies less a 50% literary discount."

A *literary discount!* I nearly burst out laughing. The man has a great sense of humor.

The old lady and Pursewarden said, and they did this in perfect harmony, "You're hired."

"What's our strategy?" the old lady asked. "Obviously you have to visit the twenty three literary characters in prison, and they have to agree that you represent them. At this point, I'd think they already have court-appointed lawyers working with them. You have to find out what has happened so far. Apart from all that, what is our strategy?"

"Why did the police enter your apartment? Who were they after?" Matt asked.

"They were after me," I replied. "One of the police officers shot at me."

"Did you shoot at him first?"

"I didn't. I didn't even have a gun."

"That's good."

"Why is that good?" I asked.

"It could come handy. We could accuse the police of attempted murder, police brutality, that kind of stuff."

The real lawyer looked at his literary colleague and partner, and I could see what he thought: in real life things are a bit more complicated. Turning towards me he asked, "Why do you think they were after you?"

I decided to be honest, "I've killed twenty rapists, give or take a few, in the past ten or so years."

There was a long silence and the two lawyers looked at me, stunned. The old lady was the first one to say something. "I know about that. Don't worry about it. These were good deeds, even Jesus said so. Don't worry about the bastards you got rid of, they deserved what they got, and the only question one could ask is why you didn't dispose of more of them."

Her lawyer looked at her with an expression of shock and bewilderment and asked, "Irene, did you hear what you just said?"

"I certainly did and I'm happy to repeat it."

"Well," the man of the law said, "in that case, let's not worry about these twenty or so murder cases; in fact, let's just pretend this conversation never took place. Okay?"

"Why?" I asked.

"Because it is likely that the police knew nothing and still know nothing about your murderous past."

"So why did they enter the apartment then?"

"They thought you had killed someone else."

"Whom? I didn't kill anybody else. I'm a peace-loving man and the rapists that I have killed, I killed each one of them very humanly. They didn't suffer, they didn't even feel a thing."

Again there was silence in the room, before I asked, "Who do the police think I have killed?"

The old lady's lawyer replied, "They thought – but they don't think that any longer – that you had killed the owner and the manager of a printing factory in Brooklyn. I know about this case because late yesterday, I received a phone call from a man in prison. He told me everything that's known about this case. He admitted to the killings and asked me to defend him. The police are no longer after you."

"So our twenty three friends are in prison only because of that little fight in my apartment?" Irene asked. "There is no other case as far as they are concerned, in fact, as far as we all are concerned, right?"

"As far as I'm aware, yes."

"Well then, let's go and get them out."

This is what happened next. The six of us – the old lady, her lawyer, the Lincoln Lawyer, June, Pursewarden and I – went to see the prosecutor who was in charge of our friends' case. When we arrived at the prosecutor's office, we were told the prosecutor was in a meeting, but it could be arranged for us to see him the next day in the afternoon at three pm. For the former Lincoln Lawyer, now called Matt, and for Pursewarden, this was not good enough. They walked into the prosecutor's office. As they had correctly suspected, the prosecutor was not in a meeting. He was reading a magazine, which he quickly put into a drawer in his desk. "You shouldn't read that porn stuff," Matt said to him. "Porn stuff?" Pursewarden asked. "Can I have a look at it?"

A few minutes later three security guards entered the office and Matt and Pursewarden were led away in handcuffs.

As these events took place, the remaining four of us stayed in the waiting area outside the prosecutor's office. "Don't follow," the old lady said, "let's just see what's going to happen." Her lawyer nodded. A few seconds later he added, "They may be successful, who knows."

"I don't think so," Irene replied. "I think it's more likely that we have to bail them out as well." She was right. But in all fairness, it has to be added, Matt and Pursewarden were successful, albeit not the way they had hoped they would be.

After they were led away in handcuffs, the prosecutor asked the four of us to join him in his office. I suspect it was the fact that one of us was an elderly lady, a circumstance that suggested to him that it might be better to listen to us instead of reading about our concern the next day in *The New York Times*. This is what New Yorkers sometimes do. If they don't succeed with the authorities they go to *The New York Times* or to CNN or to both. He didn't know why we were there, so it was better for him to be cautious.

From then on, June and I were bystanders, and the old lady and her lawyer did all the talking. A lot of what they were talking about sounded to me like etymological legal mumbo jumbo. My thoughts were jumping around a bit. Most of the time, I focused on the discussion that was going on, but every now and then I wondered why the police didn't walk into the room and arrest me for being a murderer. Aside from those intrusive thoughts, my mind also wandered and whenever I looked at June I found myself fascinated by her beauty. She looked like young Brigitte Bardot and Jane Fonda combined, very lovely and very sexy. Several times, I felt like asking her if we should go away for an hour or two, perhaps go to a hotel and make love. Each time it occurred to me at the last moment that the timing might not be good for such a tryst, and I kept my desire to myself.

After an hour, the prosecutor was joined by the Police Commissioner and the Deputy Prosecutor. I was impressed by Irene's legal knowledge, her negotiation skills and stamina. After three hours, she still sounded as fresh and sharp as at the beginning.

The old lady and her lawyer's strategy was mind-blowing. When we entered the prosecutor's office I anticipated that we might be there for an hour, hardly longer. I mean how much legalese can you produce in a case concerning twenty three crazy people who had a fight with half a dozen police officers? Of course, Irene and her lawyer realized this and therefore moved the discussion away from legal aspects towards philosophical ones.

They had decided to stick with the story that the twenty five (they also included Matt and Pursewarden now) were not people in the natural sense, but literary characters. Therefore, they argued, the laws of the United States of America may not be able to adequately deal with this case.

However, they accepted without hesitation, that they now had to explain how the existence of real life literary characters in the middle of Manhattan was possible. And it was at this junction that the discussion became highly philosophical. Fortunately – very fortunately – the prosecutor, his deputy, and the commissioner of police were philosophy aficionados. They were also friends, and it was not unusual for them to sit together for hours and speculate about God, the devil, religion, time, the world and how everything is intertwined.

38

The prosecutor said, "I accept that one could debate your argument that the law of the United States of America, as it stands now, may not apply in every respect to literary characters. However, prior to such a debate, you would have to prove the physical existence of literary characters in New York. I have no difficulty in accepting the imaginary existence of literary characters in this city, but their physical appearance is a different story."

The old lady took a deep breath. Her lawyer looked uncomfortable. June, I noticed, was about to get up and say something. She probably wanted it to be known that she, too, was a literary character. I put my hand on her arm and shook my head, indicating that this was not a good time to interfere.

"Fair comment," the old lady said. "To start off, let me ask you a question, did any of you have a dream least night that you still remember?"

For a while, there was silence, and I had the feeling that not one of the three gentlemen wanted to talk about their dreams. Maybe they regarded their dreams as something of a private nature. The old lady didn't help them. She said nothing and waited for an answer. She knows how to negotiate, I realized. The first one who talks has lost, or so the saying goes.

Although in this case, it would have been too early to talk about winners and losers.

The commissioner of police was brave enough to say, "I had a dream last night that I still remember."

"What was the dream about?" Very good, I thought. Irene asked directly without any introduction or apology. There were only two options now for the commissioner, talk about his dream, or say that he didn't want to talk about it. The latter would have made him look a little stupid because in this case, he would have been better off if he had kept his mouth shut from the beginning. I knew that he would either tell us about his dream or make up a story about a dream.

"It was a bizarre but entertaining dream," he started, "and it took place just before I woke up. I found myself in a street with very neat one family houses lined up along the side of it. In one hand, I had a tin of paint and in the other a paint brush. I remember vividly, the paint was a nice golden yellow, and I used it to paint the letterboxes in front of the houses. If a man with a big black dog hadn't appeared, I'd probably have painted every letterbox in the street yellow.

"The dog barked and the man said to the dog, 'Get him!' I clutched for my gun and discovered that I didn't have a gun. The dog jumped at me, and I grabbed it with both hands around its neck. I remember the dog's teeth injuring one of my hands." He looked at his hands as if he felt a need to check whether or not they were actually hurt. "Then the dream ended or I woke up."

I wondered whether everything he had told us was true. From watching him, I had the impression that the story with the letterboxes he painted was true, but the part where he grabbed the animal with both hands around its neck, I wasn't so certain about. He told that part just a little undecidedly. Perhaps he didn't want to admit that he was running away. On the other hand, when he checked his hands for an injury, he seemed spontaneous and sincere.

The old lady asked him, "When you fought the dog and the dog injured you... if during that event, someone had told you that what was happening wasn't real, it was just something you imagined, how would you have reacted?"

"Ha!" the man replied, "I can see what you are driving at. But well, to answer your question, I wouldn't have believed a word because I knew damn well that that dog was as real as a dog can be."

I've never been particularly interested in philosophy, but now I wondered where the old lady would go next. Just because the commissioner of police wouldn't have accepted that he was dreaming, if someone had told him in his dream that he was dreaming, did not explain the physical existence of literary characters in New York.

"Okay," Irene continued, "there was no way for you to convince yourself that the imagined dog wasn't a real dog." She looked intently at the man. "Can you be certain that I'm real, at this very moment, and not a product of your imagination?"

The commissioner of police saw the question coming and replied without hesitation, "I can't be certain in an absolute sense. This meeting could be a dream, but realistically, the world I'm living in would drive me nuts if I questioned if every moment of my life was real or imagined."

"That's very true. But in the ultimate analysis, I believe you would agree that there is a possibility that you are the only person in existence in this room, perhaps even in the entire world. I also think you would agree that everything that you experience at every moment in your life could be imagined."

The commissioner replied, "That's an undeniable philosophical truth. And the same of course applies to everybody, including to you and everybody else in this room."

"Only if everybody else in this room exists," the old lady added immediately. "If you are the only existence and if everybody else in this room is a product of your imagination, then this undeniable philosophical truth obviously applies to only you."

I could see the commissioner was uncomfortable. This was not a typical professional conversation.

"That's logic, isn't it?" Irene added.

I quickly glanced at the other people in the room. The prosecutor and the deputy prosecutor whom I had expected to jump to the commissioner's defense both seemed lost in their own contemplations. Irene's lawyer looked troubled. Maybe he had just realized that the logic presented during the past few minutes could also mean that he is the only existence in the world. Not an easy thought to come to terms with. June smiled as if she knew something the rest of us didn't.

As far as I was concerned, I understood the logic of what was being discussed, but at the same time, I thought this was all a lot of hogwash. I also thought it was quite impractical for resolving real life issues.

The old lady must have thought otherwise. She was here to solve a real life concern of literary proportions: to have the twenty five literary characters released from jail.

39

"Let's have a break," the prosecutor said. "It's almost dinner time, and I think we all could do with a bit of food in our stomachs."

"Good idea," the commissioner of police agreed. I suspected that he hoped that this might also mean a change of topic.

The prosecutor arranged for someone to drive us in a comfortable SUV to the Waldorf Astoria Hotel. He walked straight to one of the restaurants, where he was greeted like a friend, and it became obvious that he felt at home. Turning to Irene, he said, "The mayor has a tab here. I'll arrange for whatever we spent to be added to his bill. I trust this will be okay with everybody."

A few minutes later, we received the menus, and the prosecutor ordered a few bottles of wine. He didn't need a wine card to make his decision. I guess he could just as well have said, 'The usual' and the two waiters who served us would have brought exactly the same wine. This man knew the place and the place knew him.

I forgot what everybody had ordered. I forgot what I had ordered. It was all delicious, I thought. We each had three courses. The prosecutor ordered a few more bottles of his favorite wine, and during the last one or two hours we sipped coffee while enjoying each other's company.

As a rough estimate, I think we spent six or seven hours in the restaurant, although it didn't seem that long. The old lady single-handedly discussed with the three New Yorker law enforcement officials philosophical ideas and topics ranging from what Plato and Socrates supposedly had said a few hundred years before Jesus was born, to stuff that you can read about in books written by such heavyweights as Rene Descartes, Gottfried Leibniz, Hegel, Nietzsche, Russell and Wittgenstein. Not to forget, Kierkegaard and Schopenhauer were also mentioned.

A lot of what was said didn't make sense to me at all. Actually, I doubt that it made any sense at all. Or maybe, I'm just not educated enough for that kind of stuff. Either possibility is okay with me.

Despite the substantial amounts of wine that I had consumed, I noticed that the old lady consistently redirected the discussion to one particular topic: *Is the existence of matter logically possible?* What a question! Just touch the table, and you know that matter exists. But as the evening progressed, I started to realize that things aren't necessarily what they seem.

Then, in the context of this question – *Is the existence of matter logically possible?* – the discussions went in different directions, but always returned to one central topic: the Big Bang. It was not until about half way through the evening that the old lady said, "Gentlemen, you have to make up your mind. In your considered opinion, did the Big Bang ever take place?" The three gentlemen knew exactly what would be expected of them in the event that they decided that the Big Bang indeed took place. They would have to provide a logical explanation of how it occurred.

The Big Bang theory is the brainchild of Edwin Hubble. I didn't know this when dinner started, but I knew it several hours later. Mr. Hubble lived from 1889 to 1953. According to his theory, which I may add, has been further polished in the meantime by other experts, prior to the Big Bang there was nothing. What exactly that means, *nothing*, nobody knows. *Nothing* does not mean nothing, as we understand the word today. If you imagine the universe without galaxies, suns, planets, black holes and whatever else there may be floating around – an empty universe – that would still not mean that there is nothing. There would still be the universe, albeit an empty one. Prior to the Big Bang, there was no universe, there was, well and truly, absolutely *nothing*, and we don't know what that means.

Then, so the experts tell us, roughly 14 billion years ago, the universe jumped into existence out of this *nothing*. Apparently, there was suddenly a singularity. A singularity is something so small that it can't be split into two. A singularity is so small that for all intents and purposes, it can't exist. Nevertheless, suddenly there it was: a singularity in the middle of *nothingness.* Or, you could say, suddenly there was another *nothing* in the center of the previous *nothing.* I'm serious, that's what most physicists are convinced of.

Then one day (actually, there was no time yet either, so ignore that please), this *nothing* in the middle of another *nothing* exploded. Or maybe it didn't explode, maybe it just expanded very rapidly. The experts do not agree on this detail. But as it exploded or expanded, it created the universe, that's something most are pretty certain of.

They don't know what had happened at the beginning, but they think they have a pretty good idea about what had happened a second after the beginning. *Imagine!*

Anyhow, I don't want to bore you with this longer than necessary. To return to the discussion between the old lady and the three philosophy aficionados, the three knew exactly that there was no way they could explain logically and convincingly that the Big Bang indeed ever occurred.

Lawyers, politicians, and amateur philosophers as they were, they declared unanimously that it was more logical that the Big Bang did not occur than that it did occur. This way they did not have to try and explain something that can't be explained, or at least something they were incapable of explaining. Smart decision, I would say.

"Good," said the old lady. "We agree that most likely the Big Bang did not occur." Nobody said anything that sounded like disagreement. I waved to a waiter and asked him to fill up our glasses. "This time right to the top," I told him, "not only half full." He looked shocked, but I think he got over it. As the waiter did what I had asked him to do, I looked around. The old lady looked like a poker player. Her countenance gave nothing away. Her lawyer looked lost. If he had been dropped off a helicopter in the middle of Africa; he could not have looked more lost. June looked as she always does, gorgeous.

The prosecutor said, "Good thinking."

"What?" I'm not sure who said it, probably me.

"To fill up the glasses right to the top."

"Makes sense, doesn't it?"

"Sure does."

"Back to the Big Bang that didn't occur," the old lady continued. "What is the most important development that supposedly followed the Big Bang?" she asked. Without waiting, she answered her own question. "The Big Bang supposedly created the universe, the galaxies, the suns, the planets... All matter in the universe originated out of the Big Bang."

"So where does that leave us?" asked the deputy prosecutor.

That's the difference, I thought, between the deputy and his boss. The deputy asks stupid questions, the boss knows when to shut up.

"Where does that leave us?" the old lady repeated. "It leads us to the next logical conclusion: matter does not exist."

"And how do you explain the obvious fact that we are sitting on chairs in front of a table?"

"We are not sitting on chairs in front of a table," the old lady answered.

"Yes we are!" the deputy prosecutor insisted. "Touch the table in front of you, and you'll see. If there were no table, you wouldn't feel it."

"There is no table and you don't feel one."

At this point, surprisingly, the commissioner of police came to the old lady's assistance. He said, "There is only imagination that makes you think there is a table and that makes you think you can feel a table."

"Whose imagination?" I thought that was a good question by the deputy prosecutor.

"That we can't be certain about," the prosecutor replied. "It could be yours, it could be mine, it could be anybody's imagination in this room."

"Could it also be," and this time it was June who had decided to get involved, "that it is a combination of all our imaginations together, perhaps even a combination of all the imaginations of all people and all creatures on this planet."

"Even that can't be excluded," the prosecutor answered. "Although," he quickly added, "I can't really imagine that."

"Maybe all our imaginations are predetermined? Maybe the imaginations of all people and creatures in the world are predetermined?" June commented and looked around, clearly expecting to receive an answer. But nobody complied.

For a while, everybody followed their thoughts, or maybe just didn't think at all, as was the case with me.

It was after midnight when the prosecutor summed up the discussions of the day, "We haven't arrived at a conclusion as far as the twenty five so called 'literary characters' are concerned, although I think we can safely say that their existence, assuming they do exist, would be not more mysterious than our own existence. If we exist as imaginations of some kind, why shouldn't it be possible for them to exist in a similar fashion and even mix with us?" He looked around for a few seconds and continued, "Let's sleep here in the hotel tonight and try to finish this discussion tomorrow at breakfast. Is everyone amenable to that suggestion?"

"Certainly," the old lady replied.

"The bill goes onto the mayor's tab," the prosecutor said as he got up. There was a big grin on his face. He seemed to enjoy himself. "See you all tomorrow, say nine o'clock?"

"Nine o'clock it is," someone said. Could have been me. Could have been any of us, perhaps with the exception of the lawyer who looked truly depressed.

40

June and I took a room together. We made love for an hour or so before we fell asleep. June woke up at a quarter to eight. She kissed me, pulled up my eyelids and suggested that we have a shower, make love again, and then go to breakfast. We did exactly what she had suggested.

We arrived at the breakfast table five minutes after nine o'clock. The old lady was the only one who had arrived before us. "Hope you had a good night," she said. "We sure did," June replied. "How was your night?" I asked. "Couldn't have been better," Irene answered.

Within five minutes, the others arrived. Everybody looked well rested, and I looked forward to the breakfast and whatever the time ahead would be all about.

After we had ordered, the commissioner of police turned to June and said, "I think I have seen you before, I mean before yesterday. Is that possible?"

"Maybe you saw a photograph of me."

"Where would I've seen that photograph?"

"Perhaps in a book."

"What book would that have been?"

"Perhaps a biography of my husband."

"And who would that have been?"

"That would have been Henry Miller," the prosecutor answered quietly.

"You won the first prize," the old lady commented.

"So," the commissioner continued a bit hesitantly, "does that mean you, too, are a literary character?"

June just smiled at him.

"What about you?" the commissioner said and turned towards me.

"I'm as real as you, whatever that means," I replied.

Turning back to June, he said, "Forgive me if perhaps my next question doesn't sound quite right. Do you have blood in your body just like the rest of us?"

"There is nothing wrong with that question," June answered and opened her handbag. She took a safety pin out of her bag and stuck the pin, just a little, into one of her thumbs. A second later a drop of blood formed on her thumb.

"Can I have that?" the commissioner asked.

"Sure."

The commissioner took a tiny bottle, a kind of test-tube with a lid, from a pocket in his jacket, and together with June's help, managed to transfer a few drops of blood from her thumb into the bottle.

"Can I have also a drop of your blood?" he asked me.

"No," I replied.

"Why not?"

"I don't want to incriminate myself."

"Fair enough."

"What about you, Irene?" he asked the old lady.

"Same answer," she replied.

He nodded and for a moment, it seemed that this sudden and somewhat surprising topic had come to an end. Someone else at the table asked, "Can I have a drop of your blood?" This time the question was asked by the lawyer and directed towards the commissioner of police.

The boss of New York's police force looked surprised, just for a moment, before he answered, "No."

"May I ask why not?"

"You may."

"Why not?"

"Because I, too, don't want to incriminate myself; I guess just like everybody else at this table with the exception of June."

"Fair enough," the lawyer replied. He then added, "If I understand you correctly, I guess you mean that applies to everybody else at the table, irrespective of whether their blood is of a real nature or a literary nature?"

"You are spot on." But then the commissioner couldn't help himself and had to ask the lawyer, "What about your blood?"

"Exactly the same, you can't have it."

"My God," June said with a sigh of exasperation in her voice, "I'm having breakfast with a bunch of crooks."

"No, no," the prosecutor corrected her friendly. "Nobody at this table is a crook, but everybody at this table has the potential to be a crook. From a legal perspective, that's a very important difference."

The commissioner of police made a phone call. Five minutes later a police officer arrived and the commissioner gave him the vial containing June's blood. "Comprehensive analysis type A12," he said. "Tell them to phone me when they have it. Shouldn't take them more than an hour." Nobody at the table bothered to ask about the meaning of A12.

Turning towards us, he continued, "I should get the result before we're done here. I thought you might be as interested in it as I am."

"You should have asked for my permission first," June told him.

"Yes…" he agreed. "Would you have given your permission?"

"On the condition that you shared the result with me."

"Thank you."

"And on the further condition that you release my twenty five friends."

The prosecutor laughed and said, "I think Mrs. Miller knows how to force an issue."

"I shall see what can be done," the commissioner replied and looked just a tiny bit unhappy.

We enjoyed our breakfast, and it was not until towards the end that the old lady asked, "How close are we to arriving at a decision?"

The prosecutor seemed to have been waiting for this topic to continue. He replied, "As I see it, we agree that the question of whether or not, or to what extent, the law applies to literary characters is an untested question and would probably have to be decided by the Supreme Court. We also agree that it is logically feasible that only one of us exists and that everybody else and everything else is a product of the imagination of the one who exists. If this is the case, we don't know who that lucky one may be."

"The lonely and God-like one," the commissioner of police threw in.

"Quite right," the prosecutor agreed, "but things are considerably more complex. We also agreed that the existence of matter is illogical, and consequently the one amongst us who does exist, is most likely immaterial, in other words: is *imagination.* "

"Whereby, this conclusion of yours," the old lady added, "that the one amongst us who does exist, is most likely *imagination*, is something we have not yet debated."

"That's correct," the prosecutor agreed, "and I guess this is what we should talk about now."

"It could mean that the one of us who exists in the form of *imagination* is God," June concluded in awe.

"Okay," the prosecutor continued. "Let's pursue this thought. It could mean that the one of us who exists, exists in the form of *imagination*, but in the form of a kind of *imagination* that itself is capable of imagining things: *imagination* that imagines. The question then would be, who is the source of the *imagination* that imagines? And the answer to that question could be: God. And this would mean, if, for example, you, June, are the *imagination* that imagines us and the world, you could call yourself *God's imagination* or: the *goddess imagined by God*. How does that make you feel?" The man smiled and I admired both his brilliant thinking and his humor.

For a moment there was silence. Then someone said, "This is fantastic!" It took me a moment to realize that that someone was me. I continued, "If these conclusions are correct, then I do hope indeed that the *imagination* that imagines things is June."

"Why?" the prosecutor asked.

"It would mean I made love to a *goddess* last night."

I don't know why I said that. It just came out of my mouth. I looked around. The prosecutor and the commissioner of police looked amused. The deputy prosecutor was trying to make up his mind about what he should think. The lawyer looked as if he couldn't care less, which, I admit, impressed me. The old lady remarked, "Sex is a bit overrated these days, don't you think so?"

Everybody laughed except June. Looking at me she said, "You are worse than Henry."

"Sorry."

"Good intermezzo," the prosecutor said. "The crazy thing, of course, is that this is how it could be. June could indeed be *God's imagination.*"

"The odds are against that," the old lady said. She spoke more to herself than to anybody at the table.

"Why are the odds against me?" June protested. "What would be wrong with me being that close to God?"

"If Henry found out about this, he would roll over in his grave," the commissioner of police said with a perfectly straight face. "Imagine, he was married to a *goddess* and allowed the marriage to end in divorce. But," turning to the old lady he continued, "why are the odds against June being the number one amongst us?"

"On second thought," Irene corrected herself, "the odds are in her favor. She is the only one amongst us who admitted that she is definitely different. She is a historical character, the woman who married Henry

Miller, then Miller made her a literary character, then the historical character died, but the literary one continued, and now, she returned as a fusion of both. Does that make sense?"

"A bit spooky," if you put it like that," June replied.

"Everything we talked about for the past – how long? – nearly twenty four hours, is a bit spooky," the deputy prosecutor contemplated.

I could see that everybody agreed with this sentiment. He was right. We were talking about stuff that was *far beyond* the comprehension of most human beings. This is just a lot of hogwash, I thought once more, when I heard the old lady say exactly what I thought.

"It could well be that this is all just a lot of hogwash. On the other hand, the fact that we discussed these very impenetrable topics indicates to me that we were meant to discuss them. Humans can, and should, discuss the unfathomable, the inscrutable and the mysterious. This is what we did and this is what helped us to understand that we should not take one single aspect of our existence for granted, in whichever formula or identity this aspect may present itself.

"From a logical perspective, it is quite likely that things are not the way they seem. From a practical perspective, the way we experience life day after day, things are exactly the way they seem. And finally, there are very powerful people who would happily put each one of us into a home for lunatics if we argued our case for or against the release of the twenty five literary characters along the lines of our immensely stimulating discussion."

"What are saying?" the commissioner interrupted.

"This discussion was our discussion, for our benefit and to assist us in arriving at a decision, without a need to ever have to justify this decision towards anybody else. That's how I see it. That's what I am saying. What do you think?"

I thought, Irene had summarized the situation brilliantly.

The prosecutor looked towards the commissioner of police. They both knew the time to make a decision had arrived. I noticed that the commissioner's face implied agreement, probably agreement with what he felt the prosecutor's decisions would be.

The prosecutor was just about to reply to Irene's speech, when the commissioner's iPhone rang. He answered the call by stating his name. He listened for the next four to five minutes without saying one word. Then he said, "Thanks," and ended the call.

Nobody said a word. The commissioner looked around. Turning to June, he said, "I received the result of your blood analysis. Is it okay with you if I tell everybody at the table the result?"

"Please, go ahead."

"Your blood is normal human blood, with one exception. The helixes that represent your DNA and that provide an indication of your age and general health, are so damaged that you cannot be alive."

"Very interesting," someone said.

The commissioner continued, "The person who explained this to me said that every time when our cells split and in the process renew themselves, the DNA helixes experience damage. This is called aging. According to the damage done to the helixes of your DNA, I'm sorry, but you should have died several decades ago."

"No need to apologize. I *did* die several decades ago," June said calmly.

"Decision time," the prosecutor said. "Unless I hear a voice to the contrary, we unanimously agree that the twenty five literary characters are to be released and that all records of their arrests and other references to their existence will be deleted from all databases and removed from all files."

There was no voice to the contrary.

41

Nobody felt like leaving the breakfast table. For the next few minutes, no word was spoken, and everybody seemed comfortable with the ongoing silence. Like a group of friends, I thought. Shouldn't the old lady, June, and I hurry up and get the twenty five literary characters out of jail and find a place for them to stay? I didn't feel a sense of urgency for this to happen and obviously Irene and June didn't either.

The commissioner of police said, "They have an incredibly delicious Italian almond tart here, nothing like you have ever experienced before, unless you have lived in Italy. How about a piece of it with an extra strong Mocha?"

"Sounds like a brilliant idea," Irene said. I noticed that even her lawyer, who had been the quietest of all of us, seemed to wake up and show renewed interests in his surroundings.

The commissioner of police placed the order.

There were a few more minutes of silent contemplation before the prosecutor asked June, "How do you get back into your literary world?"

June didn't reply and I said, "That's a problem that still needs to be resolved. For her to return, she needs the book from which she originated."

"Which book is that? Henry Miller wrote quite a few books."

"She decided on *Sexus*."

"I see."

"The problem is," I continued to explain, "it can't be just any copy of *Sexus*. It has to be a copy of the revised edition of which we've spread thousands of eBook copies around the world and of which we've had also printed two hardcover copies. What June needs is a paper edition of the new edition of the book, ideally located in a library or in a quiet room. We had two such copies, one in Irene's library and one, which was meant to be a backup copy, in one of my rooms. But that's all gone; destroyed by the fire in Irene's apartment."

"So, what's the solution?"

"We need to print at least one new paper edition of *Sexus*."

"That shouldn't be a big problem," the prosecutor commented.

"Hopefully not, but it looks like a bit of a challenge and a lot of work. We have to do the same for the other twenty four literary characters.

Unfortunately, the computer that contained the files of the new versions of the books was in the apartment and was also irreparably damaged in the fire. The Lincoln Lawyer is the only one who should be okay. He lived with Irene's lawyer," I explained.

"Well, I guess, we all have our work cut out for us."

"We sure do," I said.

For a few minutes nobody spoke.

"What's waiting for you when you're back in your office?" I don't know why I asked this question. Probably because the prosecutor had shown interest in my undertakings.

"This and that," he replied.

"Nothing major that stands out?"

"We have a serial killer in Brooklyn."

Shit, I thought. I know a serial killer in Brooklyn.

"This has been going on for years," the commissioner of police continued. "He kills rapists. He could also be a she, we aren't sure, but our profiler thinks the killer is a man."

"Wow!" was all I could say, before something more meaningful popped into my surprised head and I asked, "Has this been in the media? I don't think I've ever heard of it."

"No, it hasn't been in the media," the prosecutor said. "We keep it under wraps, and we would like it to stay that way, at least for a while longer."

"Why would you keep something like this hidden from the public?" Irene's lawyer asked.

"Because the man, assuming he is a man, is providing a kind of public service of a nature which the law could not provide."

"*A kind of public service?*" I asked in disbelief. I knew that I had excused towards myself my criminal activities in such a manner many times, but to hear a prosecutor uttering these words seemed unreal.

"Look," the man said, "in the past 24 hours the seven of us have developed an understanding on a philosophical level that is rare, very rare. It is for this reason that I don't mind sharing with you what this serial rapist murder case is all about. However, if you think there is a possibility that you may like to share this story with someone else, please tell me now.

Nobody said a word. I think I also stopped breathing for a brief moment.

"Okay," the prosecutor continued. "Every day crimes occur in our crazy city that the police never hear about. Thousands, maybe tens of thousands of crimes, mostly minor ones. But some of these crimes are horrendous and amongst them the most horrendous ones are rape cases that are vicious, brutal, cruel, humiliating and cold-hearted beyond description. We don't hear about many of these cases because they are not reported. Often, only the victim, the perpetrator and one or two more people know about it. Frequently, there are rumors, but nothing concrete to go by."

"The serial killer that we are talking about has killed at least forty, perhaps as many as sixty, of these cold-hearted rapists in recent years," the commissioner of police continued.

For a moment I felt like jumping up and saying, 'Hang on! He killed about twenty, not forty or sixty.' But I managed to keep my mouth shut. Who knows, I thought, these guys may already suspect me and are just waiting for me to make such a blunder.

The commissioner of police continued, "The good thing about these murdered rapists is that they can't rape anymore. They are no longer a danger to their victims. Some of the killed rapists, our investigations showed, had raped many times before they found their well-deserved end. You can't help thinking that it would have been a good thing if they had been killed sooner rather than later."

"Can you see why this serial killer is not only a dangerous and efficient mass murderer, but also a person who performs a public service of a kind which the law could not perform?" the prosecutor concluded.

I felt like asking, 'Any idea who he could be?' But, again, I managed to keep my mouth shut.

"Any idea who he could be?" Who said that? It was the old lady. For a moment, I thought it had been me after all.

"I don't know if we want to know," the commissioner of police replied.

Once more, I didn't trust my ears and wondered if I was dreaming. Looking directly into the commissioner's eyes I said, "You can't be serious?"

"He is; he's very serious," the prosecutor confirmed without showing emotions. "Deep inside our hearts," he continued, "we don't want him to be caught. We want him to stop, but only for the sake of the law. We don't mind at all to see these mass killings remain unsolved for all eternity." As he was saying this, he was looking straight into my eyes as if I was the only person in New York for whom this message was intended.

'I'll let him know should I ever meet him.' Did I really say this or did I think it? I don't know. I'm afraid I may have said it, and I hope that I thought it.

PART 6:

The 92-year-old lady and her 91-year-old lover who killed himself at 61

42

The first two nights after their release from prison, the twenty five literary characters, the old lady and I stayed in a hotel. The Lincoln Lawyer returned to the lawyer's library. The third night and for several weeks that followed, we stayed in a holiday camp in Queens. We had hired twenty units and after a couple of days, everybody had settled in and felt all right.

I had managed to contact Geoff in Harlem. He joined us in the camp. I had hoped that he would have backup files of the revised and rewritten books and that he had taken these files with him and hadn't left them in the apartment. When I asked him, he replied, "Of course! I always make backups and store them at different locations."

"How many different locations?"

"That depends on how critical the files are. Of the revised books, I made three complete sets of backups. One set is at my place, one is in a safety box in a bank, and one is – and you won't believe this – inside one of Amazon's Cloud Drives."

"You're right, I don't believe that," I replied. I was shocked.

"The files are encrypted."

"Okay," I said. "That's not too bad, but still…"

"It makes you feel uncomfortable?"

"Very uncomfortable," I confirmed.

"Okay. I'm going to wipe out the files and store another set of backups with another bank. How's that?"

"That would make me feel a lot better. Thanks."

We had a meeting: the literary characters, Irene, Geoff and I. There was an audible sigh of relief when I told them about the backup files of the books. We talked about the next steps to be taken and agreed that Geoff and I would arrange for three hard cover editions to be printed of each book. We would place one copy of each of the twenty five books in a room in one of the units in the holiday camp. This room would be our temporary library. In about six weeks' time, we expected that the old lady and I could move back into her apartment. The insurance company, the builder, and the interior designers had all promised to pull out all stops to ensure that this deadline would be met. But, if it took a week longer, so be it, life in the holiday camp wasn't that bad.

The other two copies of each of the twenty five books were backup copies. We would store one copy in a safe with a bank and the other with a security firm. We would also make arrangements that would allow each of the literary characters to access the two backup copies of his or her book should it become necessary.

Three weeks later, only Irene, Geoff, I and twenty five books remained in the holiday camp. It had become obvious that the literary characters felt homesick. We had become good friends, but they were looking forward to returning to their own world. Even June, who stayed a few days longer and was the last one to leave the camp, realized that the New York of the early 21st century was not meant to be her home. Whilst she was in the camp, we made love every day. I promised I wouldn't go into details about it. What Henry had written decades earlier was enough. She said she would visit me.

The insurance company, the builder, and the interior designers had kept their promises and done excellent jobs. Irene and I moved back into the apartment. The place felt very much the same as it had felt prior to the fire. The furniture was different of course, but also of a light and modern style. The library did not yet comprise as many books as before, but that was only a matter of time. The most important books, twenty five of them, we had brought with us from the holiday camp.

I was reading the new version of *Sexus* and was about half way through the book when a question occurred to me; a question which I had wanted to ask the old lady several times before but somehow the time never felt right.

"Would you mind telling me a bit about your life?" I asked. "I know nothing about your past and was immensely impressed by your performance in the Waldorf Astoria. Where and how did you acquire your encyclopedic knowledge about philosophy and legal matters?"

Irene looked at me, and for a few seconds it seemed there was a bit of sadness in her face. She asked, "What would you like to hear? The long version or the sort version?"

"The long version!" I replied. "Definitely the long version."

43

A long time ago, a girl was born to wealthy parents. The girl's father was the majority shareholder in an investment bank, and the girl's mother was a celebrated singer. Apart from their daughter, they also had a son who was two years older than the girl. When the son was eighteen and the girl sixteen, the young man and his parents were murdered. At the time, the family lived in Chicago at the corner of Chicago Avenue and Grove Avenue.

The girl was brought up by an aunt and uncle who lived in the same neighborhood. They had a son who was close to the same age as the girl and he and the girl became good friends. By the time the girl was 21 and received her full inheritance, several million dollars and her dead dad's majority shareholdings in the investment bank and in a publishing company, the girl and the young man had become lovers.

Secret lovers. The girl's father and the boy's father, her uncle, were brothers. This meant the girl and the boy were first cousins and they were not meant to have a sexual relationship. They were meant to be good friends, that was okay, but they were not meant to be lovers, they were not meant to get married, and they definitely were not meant to have children.

They were aware of this. They were never married to each other and they didn't have children together. As the decades went past, the young man married several times and had several children. The girl never married and remained childless. She wasn't lonely or unhappy. She had friends and lovers and travelled the world. For several years she lived in various European cities, usually in the same cities in which her first cousin stayed, who had become a foreign correspondence for the *Chicago Tribune*. He travelled the world, first with his first wife, later with subsequent wives, one after the other, of course, and with their children.

Life was good. They were wealthy, they occupied themselves with what they enjoyed doing most, and they remained lovers all their lives. He was a newspaper man with all his heart, and she was an eternal student. Wherever she lived, she attended university courses covering subjects like history, philosophy, psychology, and law. She never bothered about exams or degrees. For her, life was about acquiring knowledge and about her love for him. For him, life was about the newspaper business and books, which meant writing, and about his love for her.

For all intents and purposes, they were married to each other despite the fact that they were never legally married. He was married officially three or even four times. She wasn't sure, and it didn't matter to her.

He loved danger and she trusted him. Totaling up the time they spent together, mainly travelling, just the two of them, often to remote parts of the world, comprised at least twenty per cent of their lives, perhaps as much as thirty per cent. His wives didn't know about her existence and never suspected that there was another permanent woman in their marriages; a woman far more permanent than each one of them turned out to be. At times, this seemed unrealistic, even to the lovers. His wives suspected him of having occasional one night affairs, and he did nothing to dispel that suspicion. Should they ever catch him with his true love, he'd simply declare her a one night mistake.

At times, he was a heavy drinker. Interestingly, he did some of his best writing under the influence of whiskey and wine. His health wasn't the best. He also experienced several accidents: two car crashes and one plane crash. But he was tough. Because of a few broken bones, one of his legs was shorter than the other. At times, he took opium to cope with his back pain. Opium and whiskey together, he joked, worked best.

According to his own assessment, he should have died at around the age of 70, in his mid-seventies at the latest. He lasted a lot longer, and the day came and he and Irene celebrated his 91st birthday. A week earlier, she had turned 92. They celebrated in a little town in Idaho, about 60 miles from Ketchum. This was the last time she saw him.

Her name is Irene.

His name is Ernest.

Was he the same Ernest who committed suicide?

Yes and no.

How could he celebrate his 91st birthday if he committed suicide at 61?

We'll come to that.

He returned by taxi the same night to Ketchum where he had a place to live and where his third or fourth wife, probably his fourth, was waiting for him. Irene stayed in a motel in the town where they had celebrated his birthday. The next day, she travelled to San Francisco. From there she took a plane to Havana, where they had agreed to meet two weeks later.

A few hours before her arrival in Havana, she could feel that something wasn't right. At first she couldn't feel her hands, next it felt as if she were sitting in a vacuum. Then she couldn't feel the seat she was sitting on, she couldn't feel the backrest of the seat, and several times when she looked down, the floor of the plane seemed semi-transparent. She didn't feel dizzy or sick. It felt rather as if at times the world was withdrawing from her. She decided to close her eyes, and she stuck to that decision until the plane had touched down in Havana.

She went through customs without difficulty, although everything seemed unreal to her and several times she suspected she was dreaming. She took a taxi from the airport to a hotel in the Havana downtown area where she had booked a room. The people at the reception greeted her in a friendly manner. She had stayed at this hotel many times during the past thirty years. She asked the manager to hit her. He refused her request. She suggested that she could hit him first to give him an idea about how hard he was meant to hit her. He replied that he would feel honored to be hit by her, but that there would be no way that he could reciprocate such an action. "This is not going to work," she said. "When you're gone, I'll ask the bell boy to give me a good smack."

"That is not going to happen," the manager replied. "I'm going to be your bell boy for now." He grabbed her suitcases and carried them to her room.

Inside the room she said to the man, "Okay, now nobody can watch us, go ahead, give me a good whack."

"Why? Why on earth do you want me to hit you?"

"I need to find out whether or not I'm dreaming."

"What makes you think you're dreaming?"

"For a start, the fact that you look semi-transparent, that I can see your heart, your blood vessels and your bones, these are just a few of the reasons that make me wonder whether or not I'm dreaming."

The manager jumped back a step or two and walked to a mirror and looked at himself critically. Satisfied that he wasn't semi-transparent, he said to her, "Maybe you should lie down and rest for a few minutes. I'll arrange for a doctor to visit you."

"That's not such a bad idea," she replied. "Just make sure the doctor is a solid one and not semi-transparent like you."

"We only have solid doctors in Havana," the manager replied.

"Good! A good solid doctor, that's what I need."

An hour later, the doctor arrived. He was an elderly man and looked semi-transparent just like everybody else in Havana. He asked her all sorts of questions, like how many drinks she had consumed in the plane, and he tested her reflexes by knocking a little rubber hammer onto her knees; first onto her right knee then onto her left knee. He was happy with the results and said her reflexes were the equivalent of the reflexes of a person half her age. She commented, "So now I'm also dreaming that I'm 46 and not 92. You're not very helpful doc."

She expected to receive phone calls from her love before he was due to arrive in two weeks. When she didn't hear from him, she assumed that he couldn't call her without making his wife suspicious. She continued to see people as semi-transparent, but after a week, she was so used to it that it didn't seem unusual to her any longer.

She knew the date and time when he was due to arrive and waited at the airport for him. When he didn't arrive, she was disappointed. She knew his phone number in Ketchum. The next day when she tried to phone him, an automated answering service replied, "The number you dialed is out of service."

She knew his place at the outskirts of Havana where he lived when he was in Cuba and where they had spent countless days together during past decades.

Here he had written major parts of *For Whom the Bell Tolls*.

Here they had made love.

She took a taxi and told the taxi driver the address. The man looked perplexed and said he had never heard the name of that street before. There were another three taxis nearby waiting for customers. They walked to these three taxis and asked their drivers if they knew the location of that street. They looked equally perplexed and said the name didn't sound familiar to them. She told them that she had been driven by taxi to that location three or four dozen times at least. Every Cuban taxi driver she had ever met knew that street. The men felt sorry for her and one of them went to a nearby public phone and inquired with the taxi company, but without success.

Something, she knew, was wrong. Seriously wrong. She remembered that it had all started a few hours prior to her arrival in Havana. What had been going on in the world at that time?

She got hold of every newspaper she could, beginning at that particular day until the current day. At first nothing unusual jumped out at her. When she worked her way through the papers the second time she slowed down and felt kind of uneasy whenever there was a report about a famous writer who had died in a shooting accident. The event took place in Ketchum, and at first the public was told by the writer's fourth wife that her husband had cleaned his rifle when he accidentally shot himself in the head. A few days later, the public was told that it now seemed certain that he had committed suicide. Almost every paper, especially American papers, had a full page report about his adventures life, about the books he had written and about his four marriages. Seven years prior to his death he was awarded the Nobel Prize in literature. At that time he was 54. When he shot himself he was 61.

Some of the parallels between the man Irene loved and was waiting for and the man who had killed himself were amazing, but obviously the two men couldn't be the same. Her love was 91. They had celebrated his birthday only a few weeks earlier. The man who had killed himself was 61.

At this point in the story, I couldn't hold back any longer and interrupted the old lady and exclaimed in utter amazement, "By heavens! You're a literary character! You are not real... Sorry, you are real of course, but in a different way. How come you are here and not back in the other world together with the other literary characters?"

The old lady paused. She took a sip from the wine in front of her, before she replied, "Yes, I'm a literary character, and I have been in this world since 1961. The writer who had killed himself in 1961, Ernest Hemingway, had created me. This I'm pretty certain about. However, there is one unresolved riddle. For me to have been able to move from the literary world into your world, there would have to have been in existence a book with me in it, with me as a 92 year old woman and with Ernest as a 91 year old writer. But nobody knows anything about such a book by the famous man who decided in 1961 in Ketchum that he didn't want to live any longer."

I agreed. "By now all his books have been published. Actually, I believe his last wife and sons have published after his death more books that were written by him than what he had published during his lifetime. I think I've read all of them and I can't recall one with a 92 year old lady in it."

"So, where does that leave me?"

"It leaves you in this world. It leaves you in limbo. It leaves you a healthy and fit 92 year old lady for many more years, decades, maybe even for centuries to come in this strange world of which we don't even know whether or not it is real and if it is real, what it is made of. Is it made of matter or imagination? We don't know. "

"So where does that leave me?" the old lady asked once more.

There was nothing else I could think of to say.

44

June had kept her promise and visited me. We made love and then went to an Italian restaurant in the Village. She stayed overnight.

The next morning, we enjoyed breakfast in the kitchen together with Irene. I told June that Irene was a literary character who had been stranded in this world since 1961.

"There must have been a book," June concluded immediately, just as the old lady and I had done. We talked about Ketchum, about the famous writer who had committed suicide there and the many parallels between his life and the life of Irene's great love. "I remember that suicide well," June said at one point. "I was still alive at that time and I was one of his fans. I read everything by him and about him that I could put my hands on."

"Henry didn't like him," I said.

"I liked him."

"If there has ever been something written by him about a couple in their nineties," I contemplated, "then it must have been an attempt by him to write his future biography in the form of a novel the way he would have preferred his life to progress."

"But then he shot himself. It's a sad story," June added.

I could feel my brain working in overdrive.

"Maybe there was never a book. Maybe all there has ever been was a book manuscript. Maybe Irene walked out of the fictional world of this manuscript into the so called real world, just the way you do it," I said to June. "And then... maybe... maybe... just before that famous writer killed himself, he burned the manuscript and with it Irene's fictional home and as a result also the possibility for her return to her fictional world."

The old lady had listened quietly to everything we had discussed. June and I looked at her. She had her eyes closed, and we could see that her thoughts returned to a time that perhaps could be called her birth. When she opened her eyes again, she said, "This is a perfectly logical explanation. This is what had happened. I remember it, albeit vaguely, very vaguely."

"You have been in this crazy world too long, much too long," I said. "It's time that we return you to where you belong, to the world that is your home."

June got up and hugged the old lady, and I could see tears in both of their eyes.

45

"Assuming that our theory is correct, why do you think he destroyed the finished manuscript?" June asked me later that day.

"We can only guess. Maybe the discrepancy between his real life and his fictional life was too painful for him to accept."

"Maybe that's why he committed suicide. But wouldn't killing himself have been enough? There was no need for him to also destroy perhaps the best book he had ever written."

"You mean even better than the books he had received the Nobel Prize for?"

"Maybe. At least a book very different from everything we know he had written."

"True."

"Do you think he was a happy man?"

"I think in his younger years he was," I replied. "From all we know, he was a very complex man. I have no idea how easy or how difficult it is for complex people to be happy."

"What about you? Do you think you are a complex man?"

"June, baby! Are you trying to analyze me?"

"Yes."

"Okay. I think of myself as a simple man. What do you think? Do you think I'm a complex or a simple man?"

"I think you are a man who has that rare talent to make complex things simple."

"Okay, but what does that make me?"

"Hard to say. Maybe you are a complex man who has that rare talent to present himself as a simple man."

"Oh, oh. Is that good or bad?"

"I think it's pretty good."

"Maybe that's where you should stop analyzing me and the world."

"Okay."

46

I had an idea of how I might be able to get the old lady back into her fictional world. But beyond that, I wanted more. What about me? I asked myself. I wanted to make sure that I, too, would one day be a citizen of the fictional world.

"Forget the manuscript that you originated from," I said to Irene a few days later after dinner. "Look at it this way. That manuscript and Ernest Hemingway who wrote it were your real parents, but they didn't cope well with life and gave you away for adoption. They were good parents who wanted the best for you. Look at it this way. Okay! Reality is not absolute. Reality is how you see things."

"Okay," Irene agreed somewhat reluctantly.

"The past decades you have been in limbo because you had to look after yourself, which at times was tough, but which also made you stronger. But now you have a chance to be adopted."

"By whom?"

"By an author who is going to write a book about you and about what has happened to you in recent months; a book that furthermore identifies your fictional 91 year old lover, the fictional 91 year old Ernest Hemingway. This should be enough for the two of you to continue where it all came to a stop in 1961. What do you think?"

"It sounds complicated."

"Complicated or not, I can see it: a book with you in it, with your great love and with the twenty five literary characters. This book will be your new home, your gateway back to the world where you originated from."

"And with you in it. Definitely with you too," the old lady insisted.

"I guess so," I agreed. It was clear to me from the moment I had the idea for this book that I would include myself. I had to! How else could I stay in touch with the beautiful literary women I had met and loved in recent months? This book was meant to be a gateway for two people: for the old lady and for myself. It was my gateway to happiness and love.

"Interesting idea," the old lady contemplated. "What title would you give such a book?"

I replied spontaneously, "I'm thinking of calling it *The 92-Year-Old Lady Who Made Me Steal A Dead Man's Car*."

"Love it!" the old lady exclaimed and laughed.

"We should celebrate," I said.

"Love that too. How about having a big glass of that Ancient Cognac you stole?"

"But that's gone... That was before the fire," I replied slightly perplexed. "That bottle exploded, melted... Gone!"

"Come on! Reality is how you see things. Remember? *That bottle is there.*"

"*That bottle is there...*"

A few minutes later, I returned with *that bottle* of Ancient Cognac.

Author's Note

Thank you for reading *The 92-Year-Old Lady Who Made Me Steal a Dead Man's Car*. I hope, you enjoyed this frolic through the world of literary fiction, comedy, crime and philosophy, perhaps even allowed yourself to be challenged and provoked by the philosophical topics towards the end of the book.

As author, I am interested in what you, the reader, thinks. As you may know, I am a self-published author. Reviews and referrals from readers like yourself, posted on Amazon, are very important. They do matter, not only for myself, but also for other readers. I would be truly grateful if you could please spare a few minutes and write and post a few sentences.

Here the link to my Amazon webpage: www.amazon.com/author/fs

Thank you.
Fred Schäfer

Principal literary characters

The principal literary characters mentioned in this book are listed below in the order of their appearance:

Pursewarden, *The Alexandria Quartet*, Lawrence Durrell

Jay Gatsby, *The Great Gatsby*, F. Scott Fitzgerald

Santiago, *The Old Man and the Sea*, Ernest Hemingway

Lady Brett Ashley, *The Sun Also Rises/Fiesta*, Ernest Hemingway

Man who had his penis bitten off, *The World According to Garp*, John Irving

Mona/June, *Sexus*, Henry Miller

Criminal, from a novel by Edgar Wallace

Walter Faber, *Homo Faber*, Max Frisch

Sabeth, *Homo Faber*, Max Frisch

Josef Bloch, *Die Angst des Tormanns beim Elfmeter*, Peter Handke

Alexei Ivanovich, *The Gambler*, Fyodor Dostoyevsky

Philip Carey, *Of Human Bondage,* W. Somerset Maugham

Iris, *The Blind Assassin*, Margaret Atwood

Jesus, *The Bible*, Numerous authors

Jean-Baptiste Adamsberg, from various crime novels by Fred Vargas

Jonah Borden, *Superior Justice*, Tom Hilpert

Lisbeth Salander, *The Girl With The Dragon* Tattoo, Stieg Larsson

Jane Bennet, *Pride and Prejudice*, Jane Austen

Rebecca and **Rachel**, characters created by Daphne du Maurier

Emma, *Emma*, Jane Austen

Anna Karenina, *Anna Karenina*, Leo Tolstoy

Sula, *Sula*, Tony Morrison

Jane, *Jane Eyre*, Charlotte Bronte

Scarlett O'Hara, *Gone with the Wind*, Margaret Mitchell

Emma Bovary, *Madame Bovary*, Gustave Flaubert

Lolita, *Lolita*, Vladimir Nabokov

Justine, *The Alexandria Quartet*, Lawrence Durrell

Catherine Bourne, *The Garden of Eden,* Ernest Hemingway

Nakata, *Kafka On The Shore*, Haruki Murakami

Mickey Haller, *The Lincoln Lawyer*, Michael Connelly

Füssun, *Museum of Innocence*, Orhan Pamuk

Florentino Ariza, *Love in the Time of Cholera*, Gabriel Garcia Márquez

Fermina Daza, *Love in the Time of Cholera*, Gabriel Garcia Márquez

The doctor's wife, *Blindness*, José Saramago

Oscar Matzerath, *The Tin Drum*, Günter Grass

Wang Lung, *The Good Earth*, Pearl S. Buck

Saleem Sinai, *Midnight's Children*, Salman Rushdie

Allan Karlsson, *The 100-Year-Old Man Who Climbed Out the Window and Disappeared*, Jonas Jonasson

Daniel Sempre, *The Shadow of the Wind*, Carlos Ruiz Zafón

Books by Fred Schäfer

www.amazon.com/author/fs

Identity Uncertain: Autobiography

Fred Schäfer is the author of more than twenty books. His autobiography is a multilayered story of his adventurous life, a thought-provoking and entertaining literary work that will continue to vibrate in the readers' minds long after they have finished reading the final page.

It contains nearly 200 photographs. The author explains his multiple personalities, he surprises, is funny, addresses unresolved issues, challenges humanity, questions the nature of reality, asks a former prime minister to negotiate on his behalf with God, writes about the girls he loved, revisits a teenage catastrophe, talks about the love of his life, and pays tribute to the people and events that made him the man he is today.

Unedited Realities

A riveting philosophical sci-fi mystery. Brilliant, creative, humorous, and provocative.

What the author says you should know before you buy this book:
This is a complicated book. Of all my books, it is the most complicated one. It is also a funny book, but—and how can I put that without offending you?—your sense of humor may not get it if the quality of your mind is mutilated due to watching too many mindless TV shows. As the title says, it is an unedited book. So, don't complain about mistakes. There could be few, there could be many. If your English is below average as mine, you may be lucky and not notice any mistakes. But whatever errors you discover, they are part of the deal. Very importantly, this book is a serious read from a metaphysical and philosophical perspective. However, sadly, most of you may not understand that; some of you, however, will. What else should you know? This book is a hell of an entertaining novel with a crazy plot. So, if the metaphysical and philosophical stuff doesn't click with you, just ignore it and focus on the plot. That should be okay as long as you don't ask stupid questions like, "Is this realistic?" The answer to that question is always, "Yes, it is!" Everything is realistic if you see it in the context of its relevant reality. You see, this is where the crazy plot and the serious metaphysical contemplations merge.

Having Coffee and Cake with the Devil in Chicago
A Philosophical Science Fiction Novel

Having Coffee and Cake with the Devil in Chicago is a roller-coaster ride of a sci-fi mystery, a thought-stimulating novel that raises questions about a future that could one day be reality.

A young woman is wondering how it can be that she is dead and alive at the same time. As it turns out, there is an explanation. On her journey to that explanation she visits places and is confronted by scenarios that physicists and philosophers alike would love to encounter and that will make readers scratch their heads in amazement. This novel is thought-provoking and entertaining. It is also very funny.

Don't Mention the FBI
A hilarious novel – intriguing, unpredictable and mysterious

Monica Shaw, her boyfriend Mick, their lover Lisa and a group of people from an obscure island north of Hawaii are drawn into a conspiracy that is initiated by Monica's mother, and developed by an FBI agent, who is known for his harebrained plans. The city on the island, where Monica and the conspirators live, is known for its strange natural occurrences, which defy scientific explanations. To execute the FBI conspiracy, the plotters have to leave the island and enter another country with fake identification paper.

The Mysterious Man
A bold and inspiring novel, a man's search for his family and past

A young man is found unconscious in a park in London. He has no injuries, no illnesses. Weeks later, the doctors still can't explain why he hasn't regained consciousness. A detective, a homeless man and a writer try to find answers to the questions surrounding him.

A widely traveled elderly man is working on his memoirs. He had left home at the age of nineteen. The decades that followed were dominated by his determination to overcome professional and personal adversities.

About half way through the book, the young man and the elderly man meet under extraordinary circumstances – they "collide", may be a better word – and seemingly unanswerable questions emerge.

One man's search for answers takes him around half the globe to Western Australia.

The Mysterious Man is a major novel that encompasses three genres: literary fiction, mystery and memoirs.

An Almighty Conspiracy
A novel, a thriller, four people doing the unexpected

A man sitting beside a detective in a bar in New York is murdered. Another man, whose warning saved the detective's life, disappears without a trace. A conman and a former Miss USA contestant form a relationship that's trusting and deceiving at the same time. The detective and an attractive policewoman, who is not influenced by people's appearances, form a relationship that changes from one extreme to another when past occurrences leak to the surface.

The events move from New York to Paris. Existing players and new players are brought together by fate. There appear to be links between crimes in New York and Paris. A mysterious man enters the scene and past events need to be rewritten. Opposing sides form, but which is the good side and which is the bad one? The conman, the former Miss USA contestant, the detective and the attractive policewoman do the unexpected.

The Invention of the Big Bang
A mysterious, thought-provoking and inspiring novel about taking risks and living life unconditionally

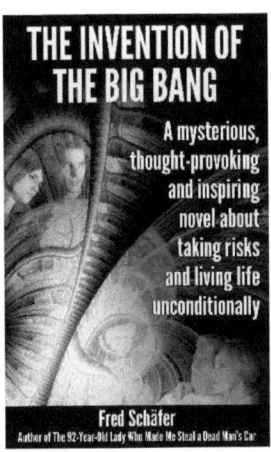

Ludwig is a wealthy banker, who wants to be an artist. His wife Gina is convinced that matter and time can't exist. Daniel and Monika, a young bohemian couple, live happy lives with values and beliefs that are in almost every aspect the opposite of what Ludwig and Gina's lives are about.

One day Ludwig starts telling Daniel his story: how he helped political refugees to escape to Casablanca; how he lost everything and what happened then; how he and Gina travelled the world. But there was more. It took a long time before Daniel discovered the banker's secret: the dark events that once dominated his past and that even Gina didn't know.

Despite all their differences, the friendship between the two unlike couples grows over many years. But then, one day, the dark parts of Ludwig's past catch up with him.

The 92-Year-Old Lady Who Made Me Steal a Dead Man's Car
A thrilling and seriously funny novel

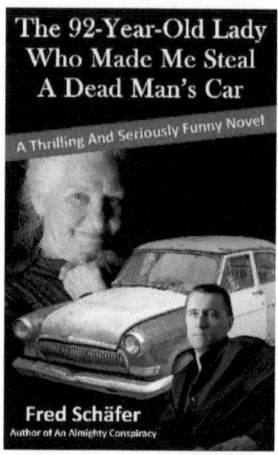

An old lady and a young man meet on a crosswalk in Manhattan in bizarre circumstances which drastically change the directions of their lives. A foul-mouthed youth is killed in a traffic accident. The old lady's apartment is visited by folks that would make most people run to their psychologist. A mass murderer explains why he thinks he is a good man. A cool Jesus asks for parts of The Bible to be rewritten. Literary characters come alive and attempt something, which would make their authors, if they knew about it, scream in horror or rotate in their graves. It takes a while for the police to get involved, but when it finally happens, the outcome is one that nobody could have predicted.

This book is Fred Schäfer's *most fictional* literary fiction novel. To fully enjoy it, it helps to let go of reality for a few hours, and float along in a world in which realism, fiction and philosophy merge into unpredictability and fun.

The Short and Wonderful Life of Henry Hemingway
A memoir of the years of fiction, a man searching for his muse

Fred's single-minded search for a muse, his struggle with his demons and his refreshingly unique literary voice make his memoirs a brilliant book, a page-turner, provocatively humorous and acutely reflective.

Henry Miller's son Tony writes about this book: *"Dear Fred, I rushed immediately to the manuscript and began reading with wild abandon. I can see clearly your influences. And I really laughed out loud about our casual meeting. You have such a good way with words. I am totally delighted by your book."*

Bruce L. Russell, Author of Channelling Henry, writes: *"Fred Schäfer takes on two of the 20th Century's literary giants. The story takes off when he arrives in New York. Miraculously, he meets an old mate of Hemingway's from the Toronto Star. He enjoys a bevy of buxom beauties, in true Miller style. Not as macho as Ernest, Fred manages to inject the book with a unique philosophy, somewhere between Schopenhauer and Bob Dylan."*

Travelling With Maria: Embracing Life
Adventures, love and happiness in India, Sri Lanka and Australia

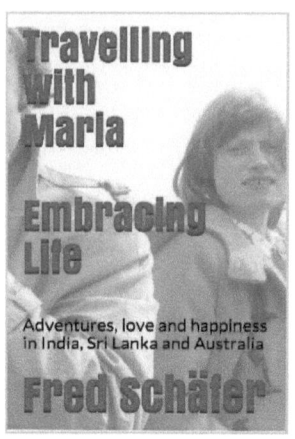

Two young people, just married, decide to sell and give away their *Habseligkeiten* (belongings) and travel the world. This was at a time when the word Internet had not yet established itself, perhaps wasn't even invented, mobile phones didn't exist and a one minute phone call from Australia to Germany cost around four dollars (today less than four cents). A few decades later, after the publication of *The Short and Wonderful Life of Henry Hemingway* – Fred Schäfer's wildly humorous and hard-hitting memoir of his years in Berlin, the USA and Canada – he writes about his and Maria's travel adventures. He surprises his readers with an enchanting and tender love story about their two year journey through India, Sri Lanka and Australia. *Travelling with Maria* is an entertaining book, a page turner, full of amazing events like running away from wild elephants, meeting a goddess in a Hindu temple, lunchtime striptease shows in an Australian pub and a lot, lot more. Ultimately, it is a book about embracing life.

How to Make Great Things Happen in YOUR LIFE
A sincere and proven approach to lasting happiness and success

What are great things in life? Money? Good health? Good relationships? Happiness? Yes, of course. And this book is about these topics. But what if the next global financial crisis makes your job and your money disappear? What if you are no longer as healthy as you would like to be? What if an important relationship becomes complicated? What if happiness seems a distant memory? In other words: what if these things turn against you? And what if as a consequence, you think, the whole world is against you? What then?

This book invites you to a journey that has a lot to do with the way you see and live your life: the way you think about life and the world you live in. After that journey – if you took your time and paid attention – nothing will be the same. Great things will happen in your life BECAUSE YOU MAKE THEM HAPPEN.

The Solution Within Yourself
Closing the gap between who you are today and who you want to be tomorrow

You have a picture of yourself and once you start changing this picture you change your entire life. The *Solution Within Yourself* is empowering and concise. Its emphasis is on thinking strategies and on how to convert these strategies into actions and results.

Top achievers differ from ordinary people in one major aspect: their minds are conditioned for success. This book will teach you how to condition your mind in whatever way you decide is right for you. You will learn rules and steps that – if you follow them – will leave you with no alternative but to achieve what you truly desire. You will learn a perception control approach that provides you with a powerful basis to deal successfully with whatever obstacles and negative events you encounter in your life. You will learn how to relax and control your emotions, even in very adverse and stressful situations.

Wendy Munro, Consulting Psychologist: "Fred Schäfer has focused on the major factors in determining the way life is experienced and created. He teaches you how to take responsibility by exploring your own belief system, the choices you have made and your attitude to life. In a very readable way Fred has addressed the human factor, the ultimate solution to Life's success or failure."

Success, Money and You
Everybody knows how to become a millionaire

This book invites you to commence your journey to financial success. It is a concise and inspiring must-read book for people who seek secure and lasting achievements: in business, professionally and financially. You will discover the philosophy of the rich, the philosophy of the poor and powerful success strategies. You will learn how to re-program your thinking and how to overcome money-making limitations. Just as you can be a good mechanic, a good accountant, a good shop assistant or whatever you are, you can be financially very successful.

DEUTSCHE BÜCHER

Das Zimmer zur Welt – Roman
Eine unmögliche Geschichte, eine unmögliche Welt, ein glaubhaftes Ende

Ein Mann befindet sich in einem Zimmer. Es ist dämmrig. Er weiß nicht, seit wann er sich in dem Zimmer befindet, wo sich das Zimmer befindet und wer er ist. Er sollte beunruhigt sein, sieht aber keinen Grund, warum der Tag kein guter Tag werden sollte. Ein alter Mann gesellt sich zu ihm. Kurz darauf befinden er und der Alte sich an zwei Orten zugleich. Das kann nicht sein. Zwei Mädchen nehmen sich seiner an. Seine Hochzeitsreise findet auf einem Fluss statt, der manchmal seine Richtung ändert. Er rettet das Leben einer Fliege. *Das Zimmer zur Welt* ist eine unmögliche Geschichte in einer surrealen Welt – und DENNOCH, eine Geschichte mit einem glaubhaften Ende.

Die andere Wirklichkeit – Roman
Eine überaus verdächtige Sache

Dieser Roman beginnt dort, wo *Das Zimmer zur Welt* endet. (Beide Bücher können unabhängig voneinander gelesen werden.) Der Protagonist der Geschichte macht eine nüchterne Feststellung: *Ich bin achtundvierzig Jahre alt und habe den Verdacht, dass ich allein bin.* Er ist nicht einsam. Er hat Freunde. Er ist sich des Widerspruchs bewusst. Unter seinen Freunden befinden sich zwei ehemalige Mönche, die aus dem Kloster entlassen wurden, weil sie Prostituierte ins Kloster schmuggelten. Er heiratet. Er entführt bedeutende Politiker und gibt ihnen eine unmögliche Aufgabe. Seine Frau und er adoptieren zwei schwierige Kinder. Er sucht weiterhin den alten Mann. Er lebt in einer anderen Wirklichkeit und hat es sich zur Aufgabe gemacht die Welt zu verändern.

Aber welche Welt? Diese Welt? Oder die Welt in der es Cafés gibt, in denen Kuchen serviert wird, den es noch nicht?

Die Beeinflussung des jungen Jakob Berg durch Henry Miller –
Roman

Im Berlin der sechziger Jahre lebt der junge Jakob Berg ein unstetes und widersprüchliches Leben. Er sieht sich als Künstler, arbeitet als Mechaniker und studiert: er schwankt zwischen den Wertvorstellungen seiner bürgerlichen Erziehung und seinen Zukunftsphantasien. Drei Jahrzehnte später, im Alter von dreiundfünfzig Jahren, liegt er im Sterben in einem indischen Ashram. Er wird von seinem Sohn Wolfgang gefunden. Jakob Berg weiß nicht, dass er einen Sohn hat. Der Sterbende erzählt seine Geschichte: von seiner Flucht vor den Gespenstern der Nazizeit, von Helga, seiner ersten großen Liebe, und davon, wie diese Liebe zu Ende ging. Jakob erzählt von seinen Vorbildern Henry Miller und Ernest Hemingway, seinen literarischen Träumen, Freuden und Qualen – von seiner Suche nach einer Muse, von der bisexuellen und mysteriösen Marlene.

Drei idealistische Bücher mit provozierendem Inhalt
Der Berg hat aufgehört zu schwingen, Zwischenbilanz und Die Aufzeichnungen

Die in diesem Band enthaltenen drei Bücher sind Fred Schäfers Erstlingswerke. Nach Alfred Nobels Testament soll mit dem Preis für Literatur ausgezeichnet werden, wer „das Vorzüglichste in idealistischer Richtung geschaffen hat". Die hier vorliegenden drei Bücher erheben keinen Anspruch auf das „Vorzüglichste", was dagegen die „idealistische Richtung" anbetrifft, da können sie sich durchaus sehen lassen.

Sie vermitteln einen beeindruckenden und ehrlichen Einblick in die Themen, die den Autor in seinen jungen Jahren beschäftigten: Kriege, Rassenprobleme, Drogenprobleme, religiöse Dogmen and Fragen, Liebe, Umweltprobleme und immer wieder stellt er die Frage, „Hat der Mensch einen freien Willen oder sind seine Entscheidungen lediglich Konsequenzen – unvermeidliche Folgen – von Vorangegangenem?" Dieses philosophische Thema zieht sich wie ein roter Faden durch die drei Bücher.

Buch 1: *Der Berg hat aufgehört zu schwingen*
Sai Baba, seine Anhängerinnen und ich
Fred Schäfer schrieb dieses Buch in der zweiten Hälfte des Jahres 1976. Es handelt sich dabei um Reiseerlebnisse, die sich 1974 in Pondicherry und Tiruvannamalai, in Südindien, ereigneten.

Auf der Rückseite der Erstausgabe dieses Buches kann man lesen: *Klar und unmissverständlich berichtet P. F. Schäfer über die Erwartungen, Vorstellungen und Ängste westlicher Indienbesucher. Hier beschreibt ein junger Autor seine Eindrücke und Überzeugungen mit einer Offenheit, die alle Lügen und Illusionen seiner Zeit, auch die eigenen, rücksichtslos aufdeckt und zur Schau stellt.*

Buch 2: *Zwischenbilanz* – Gedichte & Essays
Die Gedichte und Essays in diesem Band sind nüchterne Bestandsaufnahmen. Sie bieten Anhaltspunkte und zwingen zugleich zur Besinnung.

Buch 3: *Die Aufzeichnungen oder: Elend und Zeitvertreib eines Willens, der bezweifelt, frei zu sein*
Der Autor vermittelt mit dieser Kriminalerzählung die Problematik eines Menschen, für den mit der alleinigen Feststellung, dass der Mensch denken kann, noch längst nicht erwiesen ist, dass er für seine Gedanken – und damit für seine Entscheidungen – auch selbst verantwortlich ist.

Und was hat Johann Wolfgang von Goethe dazu zu sagen? „Geschichten schreiben ist eine Art, sich das Vergangene vom Halse zu schaffen."

Please visit:
www.amazon.com/author/fs